nF421572

THE LOST DREAM

LIRA ANZOOMA

Copyright © Lira Anzooma
All Rights Reserved.

This book has been self-published with all reasonable efforts taken to make the material error-free by the author. No part of this book shall be used, reproduced in any manner whatsoever without written permission from the author, except in the case of brief quotations embodied in critical articles and reviews.

The Author of this book is solely responsible and liable for its content including but not limited to the views, representations, descriptions, statements, information, opinions and references ["Content"]. The Content of this book shall not constitute or be construed or deemed to reflect the opinion or expression of the Publisher or Editor. Neither the Publisher nor Editor endorse or approve the Content of this book or guarantee the reliability, accuracy or completeness of the Content published herein and do not make any representations or warranties of any kind, express or implied, including but not limited to the implied warranties of merchantability, fitness for a particular purpose. The Publisher and Editor shall not be liable whatsoever for any errors, omissions, whether such errors or omissions result from negligence, accident, or any other cause or claims for loss or damages of any kind, including without limitation, indirect or consequential loss or damage arising out of use, inability to use, or about the reliability, accuracy or sufficiency of the information contained in this book.

Made with ♥ on the Notion Press Platform
www.notionpress.com

To

The GOD ALMIGHTY,without his help,this can't be written

Contents

Contents

ACKNOWLEDGEMENTS

Without support of my parents,my wife and kids this will not be complete

I

The intercom's shrill cry sliced through the pre-dawn stillness, a metallic serpent coiling around Dr. Tom's slumber. "Emergency Department," a voice rasped, "multiple fractures, trauma." The clock's luminous digits glared back at him: 2:30 AM, a time when shadows held dominion. He splashed cold water onto his face, the chill a jolt back to brutal reality. Within moments, the crisp white of his coat was a beacon in the dim corridor, his footsteps a rapid drumbeat against the tiled floor.

The emergency room buzzed with a frantic energy, a hive of hushed commands and the rhythmic hiss of medical equipment. Beneath the harsh fluorescent lights, the patient lay still, a young man twisted and broken, his life hanging by a thread. The reek of antiseptic mingled with the metallic tang of blood, a grim tableau of human fragility. The ED physician, a silhouette against the chaos, battled to resuscitate the broken form, his movements precise and urgent.

Tom's gaze settled on the patient's face, a face now contorted by pain and shock. A flicker of recognition, a ghost of a memory, stirred within him. The familiar contours, the line of the jaw, the faint scar above the brow—it was a face he knew, or thought he knew, from a life lived in fragments. A disquieting sense of déjà vu washed over him, a cold wave in the sweltering heat of the emergency room. The drunken haze that led to the accident, the broken bones, it all felt like a twisted reflection of something he could not quite grasp. The question hung in the air, silent and heavy: who was this man, and why did his face echo in the deepest recesses of Tom's memory?

The unsettling familiarity of the patient's face receded, pushed back by the urgent demands of the moment. Tom's professional mask snapped into place, a shield against the intrusive echoes of recognition. "Splints, now," he commanded, his voice sharp and clear, cutting through the ambient chaos of the emergency room. The fractured limbs, twisted and swollen, demanded immediate attention. He moved with practiced efficiency, his fingers tracing the contours of the injuries, assessing the damage.

He checked the pulses in the patient's extremities, a silent prayer for the thrum of life beneath the broken bones. "Vascularity?" he questioned, his eyes scanning the monitor for vital signs. The fear of compromised blood flow, of irreversible damage, hung heavy in the air. He palpated the patient's abdomen, searching for the telltale rigidity that signaled internal bleeding, the silent killer lurking within. A careful examination of the pelvis followed, a delicate dance between urgency and caution, seeking the subtle signs of fracture.

A collective sigh of relief echoed through the room as the initial assessment revealed a sliver of good news: the upper body, miraculously, remained unscathed. A fragile victory in the face of such profound trauma. The immediate danger lay in the shattered limbs, the potential for hidden injuries, and the ever-present threat of shock. The battle to stabilize the patient had begun, a race against time and the body's own treacherous responses.

With the patient stabilized, a fragile victory wrested from the jaws of chaos, Tom orchestrated the next phase of the battle. "Radiology," he directed, his voice firm, "X-ray and CT scan, stat." The fractured limbs, the potential for hidden injuries, demanded a clearer picture, a map of the internal battlefield.

As the patient was wheeled away, a sudden, jarring detail surfaced. Tom glanced at the patient's chart, his eyes widening in disbelief. The name scrawled across the top: Tom. A strange echo, a bizarre coincidence that sent a shiver down his spine. He, Dr. Tom, and the broken young man, also Tom.

The uncanny resonance of the shared name lingered, a disquieting undercurrent beneath the clinical urgency. He pushed the strange coincidence aside. The patient's life hung in the balance. "Duty nurse," he instructed, his voice clipped, "locate the patient's next of kin. We need to discuss his condition immediately."

The grim reality of the situation settled over him. "Immediate surgery," he stated, his voice heavy with the weight of the decision. "Multiple fractures, potential for complications. We need to act now, or we risk losing him." The urgency was palpable, a silent plea hanging in the sterile air of the emergency room. Every minute counted, every decision a gamble against the relentless tide of trauma.

The "relatives" turned out to be a trio of young men, their faces etched with worry and a lingering scent of cheap beer. "Friends," they stammered, their eyes darting nervously. "We were with him earlier..."

Dr. Tom, his professional demeanor unwavering, gleaned what information he could. Where did the patient live? Who were his family? The answers were sparse, fragmented. A new city, a transient life. Then, Rohan, the most articulate of the group, began to speak, the story tumbling out in a rush of guilt and anxiety.

"He just got here," Rohan explained, his voice thick with remorse. "Came from...Kerala, I think. Looking for a job." A flicker of recognition sparked in Dr. Tom's mind – Kerala, his own home. He pushed the thought aside, focusing on the details.

"He had a fight with his mother," Rohan continued, his gaze fixed on the floor. "A bad one. She's all he's got. His dad...left years ago. Some kind of argument, I don't know." The story painted a stark picture of isolation, of a young man adrift in a strange city, burdened by family strife.

"Tonight, she called," Rohan said, his voice barely a whisper. "They argued again, real bad. He just...snapped. Took his car, drove off like a maniac. We tried to stop him, but..." He trailed off, his eyes filled with the horror of what followed. "He hit a wall. Full speed. The front of the car...it's a mess. The airbag saved him, I guess."

The image of the mangled car, the violent impact, formed in Dr. Tom's mind. A life teetering on the edge, a consequence of anger and desperation. The shared name, the shared origin, the shared burden of a broken family – the coincidences were piling up, creating a disquieting sense of connection.

"How long have you known Tom?" Dr. Tom asked, his voice low, his gaze fixed on Rohan. The question hung in the air, a silent probe into the young man's life.

Rohan shifted uncomfortably, his eyes flickering towards the closed doors of the operating theater. "Since we were kids," he replied, his voice thick with emotion. "Childhood friends. He was born and raised here, in Noida. His mother works there."

A sense of unease settled over Dr. Tom.Noida.

"He went back to Kerala for school," Rohan continued, his voice gaining a hesitant momentum. "Secondary school, and then...postgraduate studies. He just finished recently."

The pieces of the puzzle began to assemble, forming a picture of a life lived between two worlds, a life marked by displacement and longing.

The automatic doors of the operating theater hissed open, breaking the tense silence. A nurse, her face masked but her eyes conveying urgency, addressed Dr. Tom. "Theater's ready, Doctor."

The moment of truth had arrived. Time, already a precious commodity, had dwindled to near nothing. Dr. Tom turned to Rohan, his expression grave. "We need to proceed immediately," he said, his voice firm. "He needs surgery now."

He slid the consent form across the table, the stark white paper a stark reminder of the life hanging in the balance. "You'll have to sign this," he instructed. "And you need to contact his mother. Tell her...tell her what's happened. She needs to know."

The weight of the situation settled heavily on Rohan, the responsibility of relaying the devastating news a crushing burden. Dr. Tom, his mind already racing with the intricate steps of the impending surgery, gave Rohan a brief, reassuring nod. Then, with a determined stride, he disappeared through the gleaming doors, the sterile environment of the operating theater swallowing him whole. The fight for the young Tom's life had begun.

II

The sterile environment of the operating theater hummed with a low, anticipatory energy. Dr. Tom, his mind a whirlwind of surgical procedures and potential complications, moved with practiced efficiency. He scrubbed his hands with meticulous care, the antiseptic solution a familiar, stinging ritual. The water cascaded down his arms, washing away the remnants of the outside world, preparing him for the delicate dance of life and death that lay ahead.

He stepped into the sterile zone, the air thick with anticipation, and the scrub nurse held out the pristine, folded gown. He slipped into it, the cool, crisp fabric a second skin, a barrier between him and the outside world. The ritual of donning the sterile gloves followed, a process he always found slightly irritating.

The first glove slid on smoothly, a perfect fit. But the second, as always, proved a minor battle. He inserted his fingers, the latex clinging to his skin, and then, the familiar, frustrating sensation: his middle finger stubbornly lodged in the ring finger's designated space, his little finger left awkwardly exposed. A small, almost comical, glitch in the otherwise seamless choreography of the operating theater.

A sigh escaped him, a quiet acknowledgment of his persistent clumsiness. The scrub nurse, her eyes crinkling behind her mask, offered a silent, knowing glance. With a delicate maneuver, he manually corrected the misaligned glove, shifting his fingers into their rightful positions. The small, frustrating episode was over, but it left a lingering sense of unease. Even in this high-stakes environment, where precision was paramount, his own body seemed determined to introduce a note of chaos.

He shook off the momentary distraction, his focus sharpening as he approached the operating table. The young Tom lay still, his broken body a stark reminder of the fragility of life. The monitors beeped rhythmically, a steady pulse in the tense silence. The surgical team, a well-oiled machine, awaited his command. The battle to mend the broken body, to stitch together the fractured pieces of a life, was about to begin.

The X-ray images, stark and revealing, illuminated the extent of the damage. The young Tom's right femur bore a clean, straight shaft fracture, a relatively uncomplicated break. However, the situation with his legs was more complex: both tibias and fibulas were fractured, simple but demanding careful attention. The plan was clear: intramedullary nailing, a precise technique to stabilize the broken bones. But the left leg, with both femur and tibia/fibula fractures, presented a significant challenge, requiring a delicate, multi-stage approach.

Dr. Tom, despite the unsettling coincidences, slipped into his professional persona, the seasoned trauma orthopedic surgeon. For the past five years, he had honed his skills as a senior consultant at Universal Hospital in New Delhi, tackling complex fractures with a steady hand and a keen eye. He approached the operating table with a quiet confidence, his movements precise and deliberate.

He began with the right femur, the simpler of the cases, guiding the intramedullary nail with practiced ease. The surgical team, a symphony of coordinated movements, anticipated his every need, their expertise a seamless extension of his own. They were, as he often thought, the best team a surgeon could ask for, a collection of dedicated professionals who transformed the chaos of trauma into a carefully choreographed ballet of healing.

The left leg, the more intricate puzzle, demanded a different approach. He meticulously planned the sequence of fixations, visualizing the alignment of the bones, anticipating potential complications. The challenge of stabilizing both the femur and the tibia/fibula simultaneously required a delicate balance of precision and speed. The operating theater became a space of intense concentration, a silent battle waged against the relentless ticking of the clock.

A sudden, piercing alarm ripped through the sterile silence, the monitor's insistent shriek jolting Tom's focus. The rhythmic beeping, the steady pulse of the patient's vitals, had been a constant backdrop to the operation, but now, the frantic alarm signaled a dangerous shift.

Dr. Tom's head snapped up, his gaze fixing on the monitor's flashing display. At the head of the table, Dr. Daliya, the anesthesiologist, moved with a frantic urgency. Her voice, usually calm and measured, was now sharp and commanding. She barked orders at the floor staff, her movements a blur as she administered medications through the IV line.

Tom's eyebrows arched, a silent question hanging in the tense air. Daliya, catching his gaze, offered a slight shrug, a subtle reassurance that, while concerning, the situation was under control. He trusted her implicitly, but the sudden crisis had injected a jolt of adrenaline into the already charged atmosphere.

He pushed the momentary alarm aside, his focus returning to the intricate work at hand. Time, however, had become a more pressing concern. He sped up the procedure, his movements precise and efficient, the years of experience guiding his hands. The team, sensing the urgency, worked with a heightened intensity, their movements a seamless extension of his own.

Finally, after what seemed like an eternity, the last nail was secured, the final stitch placed. The surgical field, once a chaotic landscape of broken bones, was now a testament to meticulous repair. Tom straightened, his back aching, his eyes weary. He glanced at the wall clock: 10:00 AM. Seven hours. Seven hours since the jarring ring of the intercom had shattered the pre-dawn stillness.

A deep breath escaped his lips, a sigh of relief mixed with exhaustion. He peeled off the sterile gloves, the latex clinging to his sweaty skin, a tangible reminder of the long, arduous battle. The weight of the responsibility, the fragile line between life and death, lifted slightly, replaced by the quiet satisfaction of a job well done.

III

The sterile hum of the operating theater faded as Tom stepped into the relative quiet of the recovery area. He paused, briefly, to discuss the patient's condition with Dr. Daliya, exchanging clinical observations and post-operative instructions. A sense of shared accomplishment, tempered by the lingering tension of the earlier alarm, hung in the air.

With a final nod, he thanked his team, their tired eyes reflecting the long hours they had endured. He exited the theater, the weight of the day settling upon him. He had to speak with the patient's friends, to relay the outcome of the surgery, to offer a sliver of reassurance.

In the lobby, he found Rohan and his companions, their faces etched with anxiety. He scanned the room, searching for the patient's mother, the woman who had only moments before been the subject of a heated phone call, the catalyst for the night's tragic events. "Where's his mother?" he asked, his voice low.

"She just stepped out for coffee," Rohan replied, his voice tight. "She was...she was very upset."

Tom nodded, understanding. He turned his attention to Rohan and his friends, offering a concise summary of the surgery. "The operation went well," he stated, his voice calm and professional.

"We've stabilized the fractures. He'll be moved to the post-operative care unit, the surgical ICU, where he'll be monitored closely for the next 24 hours. You can visit him once he's settled."

He paused, a flicker of something akin to guilt passing over him. "I'll be out of station for the next two weeks," he continued, "but my junior doctor, Dr. Ali, will be taking over his care. He's an excellent surgeon, you can rest assured your friend is in good hands."

The words felt inadequate, a clinical detachment in the face of such raw emotion. He wanted to offer more, to bridge the gap between doctor and friend, but the weight of his own impending departure, the strange echoes of the patient's life resonating with his own, created a distance he couldn't quite close. He left them with a final, reassuring nod, the unspoken questions hanging heavy in the air.

A brief, but thorough, handover followed. Tom met with Dr. Ali, his junior colleague, in a quiet corner of the recovery area. He detailed the patient's condition, the intricacies of the surgical procedures, and the post-operative care plan. He emphasized the potential complications, the need for vigilant monitoring, and the importance of clear communication with the patient's family.

Dr. Ali, attentive and professional, absorbed the information, asking pertinent questions and offering insightful observations. Tom felt a sense of relief, knowing the patient was in capable hands.

The Universal Hospital Group, a sprawling medical empire, had branches across international borders, including a significant presence in Uzbekistan. As a senior specialist surgeon, Tom was often called upon to consult and operate at their Tashkent facility.

Tonight, he was scheduled to depart for the Uzbek capital.

He returned to his apartment, a comfortable space provided by the hospital within its complex. It was a haven of quiet amidst the bustling medical environment. His daughter, Aswathy, was there, the familiar scent of her presence a calming balm. She had recently joined his team, a post-trauma stress counselor, her expertise invaluable in the aftermath of traumatic injuries.

Aswathy, with her gentle demeanor and keen understanding of human psychology, provided a stark contrast to the clinical detachment of the surgical world. She was a grounding force, a reminder of the human cost of trauma, the emotional scars that lingered long after the physical wounds had healed. He briefly explained the events of the night and the young patient with the same name. Aswathy listened intently, her brow furrowed in concern.

Tom's apartment, though spacious and well-appointed, held a quiet emptiness, a lingering echo of loss. He was a widower, his life shaped by the absence of his wife, who had died in a year after giving birth to Aswathy. Their marriage, arranged and brief, had lasted barely a year, a fleeting moment of happiness abruptly extinguished.

The tragedy had driven him from his native Kerala, a place now tinged with the bittersweet memories of his past. He and Aswathy had forged a life together, a father-daughter bond strengthened by shared grief. He pursued his post-graduate studies in orthopedics, building a career that took him to various hospitals in Delhi, before finally settling at Universal Hospital five years prior.

His only close relative, his mother, had passed away ten years ago. The loss had been profound, a final severing of his ties to his homeland. He had returned to Kerala only once, for her cremation, a somber pilgrimage that reinforced his detachment from the place of his birth.

The shared name, the shared origin, the shared echoes of broken families—these coincidences, now magnified by his own history, felt like a disquieting intrusion. He looked at Aswathy, her empathetic gaze a stark contrast to his own clinical detachment. He knew he had to leave for Tashkent, but the lingering feeling of something unresolved, something he couldn't quite put his finger on, weighed heavily on his mind.

IV

The hum of the jet engines was a constant drone, a white noise that filled the cabin as Tom stared out the window. The city lights of New Delhi dwindled below, a glittering tapestry against the vast, dark canvas of the night. He was en route to Tashkent, a familiar journey, yet tonight, a strange unease lingered.

The coincidences of the day—the shared name, the shared Kerala connection, the broken family, the young man's desperate act—played on his mind like a discordant melody. He tried to dismiss them as mere chance, random occurrences in the vast tapestry of human experience. But the feeling persisted, a nagging sense that something more was at play.

He thought of Aswathy, her empathetic gaze, her understanding of the human psyche. She would likely see the connections, the echoes of his own past in the young Tom's story. He, however, preferred the clean, clinical detachment of his profession, the focus on broken bones and surgical procedures.

Tashkent awaited, a city of bustling markets and ancient architecture, a world away from the sterile environment of the operating theater. He had a schedule of consultations and surgeries, a demanding itinerary that would keep him occupied. He hoped the work would serve as a distraction, a way to silence the persistent echoes of the young Tom's life.

Yet, as the plane descended towards Tashkent, a sense of foreboding settled over him. It was more than just the fatigue of the long day, more than the lingering unease of the operating room. It was a feeling, deep and unsettling, that the threads of their lives were somehow intertwined, that the coincidences were not random, but a deliberate pattern, a message he was yet to decipher. He felt that he was running away from something, but he did not know what it was.

The sterile, impersonal hotel room in Tashkent offered little comfort. Tom, exhausted but restless, made two phone calls. First, he contacted Aswathy, his voice a low murmur, reassuring her of his safe arrival. "Landed just now," he said, the static of the international call a distant hum in his ear. "Everything's fine."

Then, he dialed Dr. Ali, his professional demeanor snapping back into place. "How's the patient?" he asked, his voice sharp and concise.

"He's stable," Dr. Ali replied, his voice calm and reassuring. "Conscious, responding well. Still in the surgical ICU, but we're planning to move him to a regular room tomorrow."

A flicker of relief passed through Tom. "Good," he said. "Has he...has he seen his mother?"

"He's spoken to his friends," Dr. Ali reported, "but he's been resistant to seeing his mother. He seems...distracted."

Tom frowned, a sense of unease settling over him. The young man's reluctance to face his mother, the very person whose voice had triggered his reckless drive, spoke of a deeper emotional turmoil. The fractured bones were healing, but the wounds within, the unseen scars of family conflict, remained raw and open. He wondered what words were spoken between mother and son that led to such a destructive event.

He thanked Dr. Ali, the conversation ending with a clinical exchange of post-operative details. He hung up the phone, the silence of the hotel room amplifying the unease that lingered within him. The young Tom's story, the echoes of his own past, felt like a persistent, nagging reminder of unresolved issues, of emotional wounds left untended.

The first rays of dawn painted the Delhi sky in hues of soft pink and pale orange, a gentle awakening to a new day. In Tom's apartment, Aswathy stirred, the soft rustle of her bedsheets breaking the quiet stillness. She rose, her movements fluid and graceful, and began her morning routine.

The familiar rituals of brushing her teeth and bathing brought a sense of calm, a grounding routine before the day's demands. She chose a simple salwar and kurti, the comfortable fabric a familiar comfort. The aroma of freshly cooked idlis and coconut chutney wafted from the kitchen, a fragrant promise of breakfast. Their maid, a quiet, efficient presence, had prepared Aswathy's favorite meal, a taste of home in the bustling city.

Aswathy reached for her phone, a quick call to Tashkent to bridge the geographical distance. The time difference, a mere thirty minutes, made the morning greeting seamless. "Good morning, Papa," she said, her voice warm and bright.

"Good morning, Aswathy," Tom replied, his voice a low, familiar rumble. "How are you?"

"I'm fine," she said, a brief exchange before the day's obligations pulled them in separate directions. "I'm about to head to the office."

With a final, affectionate goodbye, she ended the call. The idlis and chutney beckoned, a comforting start to the day. She ate quickly, savoring the familiar flavors, then gathered her things and headed out, the city's vibrant energy a stark contrast to the quiet solitude of her apartment. The day ahead, filled with the complexities of human trauma, awaited her.

Aswathy's office, a haven of quiet empathy amidst the hospital's bustling activity, became a sanctuary for five young men that day. Each carried the weight of trauma, the invisible scars left by accidents, violence, or loss. She listened patiently, her gaze unwavering, her voice a soothing balm to their troubled minds. She offered guidance, tools to navigate the turbulent waters of post-traumatic stress, and a safe space to share their burdens.

The hours passed in a blur of shared stories and quiet understanding. By lunchtime, a sense of quiet exhaustion settled over her. She sought out Dr. Ali in the hospital cafeteria, a brief respite from the emotional intensity of her work.

As they shared a simple meal, the conversation turned to the patient her father had operated on. "How is young Tom doing?" she asked, her voice casual.

"He's moved to a regular room," Dr. Ali replied, taking a bite of his sandwich. "Physically, he's recovering well. But he's still...withdrawn. He barely speaks to his mother."

Aswathy paused, a flicker of concern in her eyes. "He shares a name with Papa," she said, a quiet observation.

Dr. Ali nodded. "Yes, it's quite a coincidence. And he is from Kerala, just like your father."

The coincidences, now spoken aloud, hung in the air, a subtle undercurrent beneath the clinical conversation. Aswathy felt a familiar unease, a sense that something more than chance was at play. She wondered if her father was aware of the all the coincidences.

Aswathy made a spontaneous decision. Despite her packed schedule, she felt compelled to meet the young Tom, to see him with her own eyes. The coincidences, the shared name, the shared origin, the emotional turmoil—they all coalesced into a sense of urgency.

She made her way to the tenth floor, where his room was located. The elevator doors slid open, and she stepped inside, alone. As the doors closed, she noticed the fan was still. The Delhi heat, already oppressive, turned the confined space into a sweltering oven.

The lift ascended slowly, each floor a drawn-out, stifling climb. By the time the doors finally opened on the tenth floor, Aswathy was perspiring, her clothes clinging to her skin. She stepped out, a wave of hot air washing over her.

Tom's room was conveniently located near the elevator. Inside, a duty nurse was diligently changing the patient's IV drip. The room was quiet, the air thick with the sterile scent of antiseptic. The young Tom lay still, his gaze distant, his expression guarded. There was no one else present.

VI

The world swam in and out of focus for young Tom, a hazy landscape of pain and medication. The potent analgesics, including the heavy veil of opioids, blurred the edges of reality, leaving him adrift in a liminal space between wakefulness and slumber. When his eyes flickered open, he saw a vision, an ethereal figure approaching his bedside.

She was an angel, he thought, a celestial being sent to ease his suffering. Her face was breathtakingly beautiful, a delicate balance of strength and serenity. Her hands, graceful and slender, moved with a gentle rhythm, arranging strands of hair that had fallen across her shoulders. Her eyes, deep and luminous, held a captivating bluish hue, a pool of compassion in the sterile room.

She wore a simple salwar and kurti, the fabric soft and flowing, a stark contrast to the stark white of the hospital linens. Her presence radiated a quiet warmth, a soothing balm to his aching body and troubled mind.

Her voice, when he finally heard it, was a soft, melodic whisper, a gentle cadence that resonated deep within him. He heard his name, spoken with a tender inflection, a sound that seemed to echo from a distant, forgotten place. He could not understand the words, but the sound was beautiful. The angel was talking with the nurse, her voice a soothing counterpoint to the rhythmic beeping of the monitors. For a moment, suspended in the haze of medication, he believed he had crossed over, that this beautiful being was guiding him towards a peaceful oblivion.

Aswathy observed a subtle shift in the young Tom's demeanor, a flicker of awareness returning to his eyes. He was emerging from the medicated haze, his consciousness slowly surfacing. Only his face, pale and fragile, was visible above the crisp white bedsheets. The bandages encasing his legs, stained with faint, rusty blood spots, spoke of the brutal trauma his body had endured.

Despite the pain etched on his features, an undeniable innocence radiated from him. His face, though gaunt and weary, held a youthful vulnerability that tugged at Aswathy's heart. A sudden, almost overwhelming urge washed over her, a desire to offer comfort, to soothe his pain with a gentle, maternal gesture. She felt an impulse to press a warm kiss to his forehead, a silent reassurance in the face of his suffering.

The small, wispy bits of hair that framed his face, dark and soft, added to his vulnerable charm. He grimaced, a subtle contortion of his features, a silent acknowledgment of the pain that still pulsed through his broken body. The contrast between his fragile innocence and the brutal reality of his injuries was stark, a poignant reminder of the fragility of life.

"Hello, Tom," Aswathy said softly, her voice a gentle caress against the sterile silence of the room. The sound of her voice, a gentle ripple in the medicated haze, seemed to penetrate the young man's consciousness.

Suddenly, the rhythmic beeping of the ECG monitor erupted into a frantic alarm, a jarring cacophony that shattered the quiet atmosphere. Aswathy's heart leaped into her throat, a wave of fear washing over her. The sudden change in his vitals, the insistent, urgent alarm, filled her with a sense of dread.

In a moment of instinctive panic, she reached out and grasped his hand, her fingers closing around his palm. The touch, warm and reassuring, seemed to have an immediate effect. The frantic beeping of the monitor began to subside, the alarm slowly returning to its steady, rhythmic pulse.

The young Tom's body relaxed, the tension draining away. His breathing deepened, becoming slow and even. He drifted back into a peaceful, medicated slumber, the alarm silenced, his hand held gently in Aswathy's. The contact, though brief, had created a moment of profound connection, a silent exchange of comfort and reassurance.

VII

Aswathy left Tom's room, the lingering tension of the alarm and the quiet connection with the young man weighing heavily on her mind. She returned to her consulting room, but the usual focus of her work eluded her. The images of his fragile form, the sound of the frantic beeping, and the unexpected warmth of his hand in hers kept intruding, disrupting her concentration.

With her appointments concluded, she decided to leave the hospital early. A sense of restlessness propelled her, a need to escape the sterile environment and find solace in the familiar rhythms of daily life. She decided to go grocery shopping, a mundane task that offered a welcome distraction.

The supermarket, located directly across from the hospital, was relatively empty at this hour. She moved through the aisles, selecting fresh vegetables and fruits, her purchases minimal, reflecting the quiet solitude of her apartment. With her father away, the needs were simple, only for herself and Malu Amma.

Returning home, she sought the comforting warmth of a bath, the hot water easing the tension in her muscles. She changed into a comfortable evening gown, the soft fabric a soothing touch against her skin.

Malu Amma, her ever-present companion, had prepared a plate of crispy banana fritters and a steaming cup of black tea. Aswathy settled onto the couch, the television flickering with the muted sounds of a news program. The sweet, caramelized flavor of the banana fritters, paired with the strong, bitter tea, was a familiar comfort.

Malu Amma had been a constant presence in Aswathy's life, a surrogate mother, a source of unwavering support. An orphan herself, she had found a home with Tom and Aswathy, her loyalty and affection a steadfast anchor in their lives. Her culinary skills were legendary, her ability to transform simple ingredients into comforting delicacies a testament to her nurturing spirit. As Aswathy savored the banana fritters, the quiet rhythm of the evening settled around her, a temporary respite from the anxieties of the day.

A gentle patter began to fall outside, a soft drizzle that cooled the humid Delhi air. Aswathy, drawn by the soothing rhythm of the rain, rushed to the balcony. The air, washed clean by the drizzle, felt fresh and invigorating. She told Alexa to play a playlist of Johnson Mash's soft, melodious songs, the familiar tunes creating a tranquil atmosphere.

Malu Amma followed, carrying a tray with more banana fritters and steaming cups of tea. They settled into comfortable chairs, the sounds of the drizzle and the soft music creating a peaceful symphony. The sweetness of the bananas, the warmth of the tea, and the gentle patter of the rain created a sense of serene contentment.

But beneath the surface of tranquility, a quiet melancholy settled over Aswathy. The absence of her father, the lingering anxieties of the day, and the strange connection with the young Tom created a sense of emotional vulnerability. She leaned her head against Malu Amma's lap, seeking the comfort of her familiar presence.

Malu Amma, her hands gnarled and warm, gently stroked Aswathy's hair, her touch a silent reassurance. The rhythmic caress, the soft music, and the gentle drizzle created a cocoon of comfort, a temporary escape from the complexities of the world. In that moment, Aswathy found solace in the simple, unwavering love of her surrogate mother, a quiet haven in the midst of her unspoken anxieties.

They remained on the balcony for a long time, the gentle music weaving a tapestry of sound around them. The rain had ceased, leaving behind a cool, damp stillness. Aswathy, lulled by the familiar melodies and the comforting presence of Malu Amma, drifted into a peaceful slumber.

"Mole Aswathy," Malu Amma's soft voice roused her, the familiar endearment a gentle nudge back to consciousness. Aswathy opened her eyes, the darkness of the night punctuated by the twinkling lights of the Delhi streets. She glanced at her watch: 9:00 PM.

Malu Amma had prepared a simple dinner of chappathi and sabzi, a comforting meal that Aswathy ate with quiet appreciation. After bidding Malu Amma goodnight, she retreated to her bedroom, the day's events still lingering in her mind.

She dialed her father's number, the familiar ringtone a welcome sound. Tom, having just returned from his work, answered, his voice warm and reassuring. They exchanged accounts of their respective days, a familiar ritual that bridged the geographical distance between them.

When Aswathy recounted her visit to the young Tom's room, she felt a sudden wave of embarrassment wash over her. The memory of grasping his hand, the unexpected surge of emotion, made her blush. She stammered slightly, trying to explain the incident, but the words felt clumsy and inadequate.

She had touched countless patients in her role as a counselor, offering comfort and support. But never had she felt the same sense of awkwardness, the same inexplicable blush that now colored her cheeks. Only the touch of young Tom had elicited this strange, unfamiliar reaction. She felt a growing curiosity about this young man.

VIII

The following day was a whirlwind of appointments and consultations for Aswathy, leaving her with no time to visit young Tom. Dr. Ali, however, kept her updated on his progress. "He's doing well physically," Ali reported, "but he's still very withdrawn. He refuses to speak to or see his mother."

A detail Ali mentioned resonated with Aswathy: young Tom was an only child, just like her. The shared experience of being alone in the world, of carrying the weight of familial expectations, created a sense of unexpected kinship.

As night fell, and she prepared for bed, a deep sadness settled over her, an inexplicable melancholy that she couldn't quite pinpoint. The usual comforts of her routine offered no solace. Her sleep was fitful and disturbed, punctuated by restless dreams and a sense of unease.

She woke feeling drowsy and uncharacteristically irritable. The morning's usual pleasures, the familiar aroma of idlis and chutney, failed to lift her spirits. The food tasted bland, devoid of its usual comforting flavors. In a moment of uncharacteristic frustration, she snapped at Malu Amma, her voice sharp and accusatory. "These idlis are terrible!" she exclaimed, her words harsh and uncalled for.

Malu Amma, her face etched with surprise and hurt, simply nodded and retreated to the kitchen, her silence a heavy reproach. Aswathy immediately regretted her outburst, the uncharacteristic display of anger leaving a bitter taste in her mouth. She couldn't understand the source of her discontent, the strange unease that had settled over her like a dark cloud. The young Tom, his silent suffering, and the strange connection she felt to him seemed to be the source of her unrest.

A wave of guilt washed over Aswathy as she recalled her harsh words to Malu Amma. Upon reaching her hospital room, she immediately recorded a voice message, her voice soft and apologetic, expressing her remorse and affection. The uncharacteristic outburst had left her feeling deeply ashamed.

The day's appointments passed in a blur, her mind preoccupied with the young Tom and her own inexplicable sadness. She tried to contact Dr. Ali for an update, but he was engaged in an emergency surgery. After lunch, she decided to visit Tom's room, a spontaneous decision driven by an inner compulsion she couldn't quite explain.

As she reached the tenth-floor corridor, she noticed its quiet emptiness. The suite rooms, reserved for patients requiring extra care, were less populated, creating a tranquil, almost deserted atmosphere. She glanced towards the nurses' station and saw the staff engaged in their lunch break, a silent signal that she could proceed without interruption.

As she approached Tom's room, she heard voices emanating from within. The window was slightly ajar, allowing her to hear snippets of conversation. Tom was talking with his friends.

Hesitant to intrude, Aswathy decided to wait in the corridor, her curiosity piqued by the conversation. Rohan's voice, clear and distinct, reached her ears.

"The car's a total loss," Rohan said, a hint of amusement in his voice. "If Dr. Tom hadn't intervened, you'd be a total loss too."

Tom's voice, though weak, was clear. "My mother?" he asked abruptly, his tone shifting.

"She was here all night,"

Rohan replied, his voice softening. "But she had to go to work. Her leave was over."

The mention of his mother seemed to unsettle Tom. He changed the subject, his voice taking on a dreamy, distant quality. "Yesterday," he said, "I thought I was dying. And then...an angel came. She touched my hand, and I fell asleep. When I woke up, she was gone."

He paused, his voice filled with a strange wonder. "She had a dimple," he continued, "just like my mother's."

A wave of heat flushed Aswathy's cheeks as she listened to Tom's description of the "angel." The detail about the dimple, the uncanny resemblance to his mother, sent a shiver of recognition through her. She quickly turned and retreated to her office, her mind reeling.

With her appointments concluded, she found herself alone, the quiet hum of the hospital a backdrop to her swirling thoughts. She asked Alexa to resume her playlist, seeking solace in the familiar melodies. The first song that played was the Malayalam classic, "Pranayamanithooval pozhiyum pavizha mazha," from the movie "Azhakiya Ravanan."

A blush crept up her neck as she listened to the romantic lyrics. She remembered countless car rides with her father, the song playing softly in the background. He would always skip this song, playfully claiming it wasn't his "favorite." The memory, usually a source of amusement, now felt tinged with a strange, unsettling significance.

Just as she was lost in her thoughts, Dr. Ali entered her office, his face etched with fatigue. "Long surgery," he sighed, collapsing into a chair.

"Fancy a coffee in the canteen?"

Aswathy, seeking a distraction from her turbulent thoughts, readily agreed. The prospect of a shared coffee, a moment of respite from the day's emotional intensity, was a welcome reprieve.

As they settled into the canteen, the aroma of coffee filling the air, Dr. Ali provided an update on Tom's progress.

"He's improving remarkably fast," Ali said, his voice laced with professional satisfaction. "His dressings were changed today, and we're planning to start early mobilization tomorrow."

He paused, a thoughtful expression on his face. "I was wondering," he continued, "if you'd be interested in observing his mobilization. Your presence, as a trauma counselor, could be incredibly helpful in motivating him. And, of course, as Dr. Tom's daughter, your presence would carry a certain weight."

Aswathy's interest was piqued. The opportunity to observe Tom's progress, to witness his physical recovery firsthand, held a certain appeal. "I would like that," she replied, her voice tinged with curiosity.

"Excellent," Ali said, a smile spreading across his tired face. "It would be good for him to see some friendly faces. He is still very reserved, and I am worried about his mental state. The sooner we start his mobilization, the better for his mental health too."

IX

As Aswathy made her way home, she stopped at a flower stall and purchased a string of fragrant jasmine blossoms. Malu Amma adored the sweet, intoxicating scent, and Aswathy hoped the flowers would serve as a tangible apology for her earlier outburst.

Upon arriving home, she was greeted by the familiar aroma of banana fritters and brewing black tea. Malu Amma, her face radiating warmth, welcomed her with open arms. Aswathy hugged her tightly, reiterating her apology. "I'm so sorry, Malu Amma," she said, her voice filled with genuine remorse. She then presented the jasmine flowers, their delicate white petals a symbol of her affection.

Malu Amma's smile widened, her eyes twinkling with amusement. She knew Aswathy's gentle nature, her occasional moments of frustration quickly followed by heartfelt apologies. They shared a lighthearted laugh, the tension of the morning melting away as they savored the banana fritters and tea.

After dinner, Aswathy called her father, updating him on Tom's progress and Dr. Ali's plan for mobilization the following day. "Ali wants me to be there," she explained. "He thinks my presence might be helpful."

Tom's voice, usually calm and composed, held a hint of anxiety. "Ali told me," he said. "It's...it's strange. I've never not seen a patient in the immediate post-operative period. I feel...anxious."

Aswathy sensed his unease. "He's doing well, Papa," she reassured him. "Ali's taking good care of him."

"I know," Tom replied, his voice still tinged with worry. "But...I'd feel better if you were there. Accompany Ali tomorrow, on my behalf. Please."

Aswathy agreed, understanding her father's unspoken concern. The strange coincidences surrounding the young Tom, the shared name, the shared origin, the echoes of their own family histories, seemed to have created a sense of unsettling connection for him. She felt a growing sense of responsibility, a need to understand the threads that linked their lives.

After ending the call with her father, Aswathy changed into her nightdress, seeking the comfort of familiar routines. She asked Alexa to resume her playlist, hoping the music would soothe her restless mind. This time, the 90s Bollywood hit, "Premi Aashiq Awaara," filled the room, its romantic melody stirring an unexpected blush in her cheeks. She couldn't understand her own reaction, the sudden wave of warmth that accompanied these romantic tunes.

She decided to lose herself in her book, hoping the familiar rhythm of the words would lull her to sleep. She read for almost two hours, the story weaving a tapestry of its own, but her thoughts kept drifting back to the young Tom, his fragile form, and the strange connection she felt to him.

As sleep finally claimed her, the last song she heard was "Baazigar O Baazigar," its haunting melody echoing in her subconscious. Her dreams began to unfold, a surreal blend of reality and fantasy.

She saw Shah Rukh Khan and Kajol, their iconic figures singing the familiar song, their romantic chemistry filling the dreamscape.

Suddenly, the dream shifted, the familiar figures vanishing into thin air. In their place, a boy appeared, his legs heavily bandaged, the white fabric stained with dark, ominous blotches of blood. She couldn't see his face, only the stark image of his injured limbs, a chilling reminder of the fragility of the human body.

The dream intensified, a sense of dread creeping into her heart. She tried to reach out to the boy, to offer comfort, but he remained just out of reach, a silent, haunting presence. The image of the bandaged legs, the dark stains, became increasingly vivid, filling her with a sense of panic.

She woke with a start, her heart pounding, her breath coming in ragged gasps. The dream lingered, a disturbing afterimage that refused to dissipate. The image of the boy, the bandaged legs, felt like a chilling premonition. She could not fall back to sleep.

Aswathy, still shaken by the unsettling dream, asked Alexa for the time. "It's 5:00 AM," the voice replied, the early hour amplifying her sense of unease. Sleep was out of the question.

She rose, her movements sluggish, and went to the bathroom, seeking the cleansing ritual of a shower to wash away the remnants of the disturbing dream. After calling Malu Amma, she emerged from the bathroom, her skin tingling with the warmth of the water.

Deciding to seek solace in a spiritual space, she opted to visit a nearby temple. She dressed in a vibrant red saree, the rich fabric a stark contrast to her pale complexion, and a matching blouse. She applied minimal makeup, seeking a natural radiance that mirrored the tranquility she hoped to find.

She informed Malu Amma of her plans, and to her surprise, Malu Amma promptly prepared to accompany her. The temple, a familiar sanctuary, offered a sense of peace and connection to something larger than herself.

The early morning hour meant the temple was relatively quiet, the usual throngs of devotees absent. After offering their prayers and seeking blessings, they began their walk back home. Malu Amma, noticing the vibrant red of Aswathy's saree, purchased a string of fresh jasmine flowers and gently placed them in Aswathy's hair.

The fragrant blossoms, nestled against her dark hair, enhanced Aswathy's natural beauty, her face glowing with a quiet radiance. The combination of the red saree and the white Jasmine flowers enhanced her beauty.

Aswathy entered her hospital room, a sense of calm settling over her. The morning's temple visit had left her feeling refreshed and at peace. With no scheduled appointments, she decided to dedicate the day to visiting Tom, planning to see her inpatient client in the afternoon. She settled into a chair, Alexa's soft melodies filling the room as she perused the daily newspaper.

A sudden knock on the door broke her concentration. Dr. Ali entered, his face beaming with a cheerful "Good morning." Ali was more than just her father's colleague; he was a close family friend, their only real confidante.

Seeing Aswathy in a saree, a rare sight in the hospital setting, Ali offered a sincere compliment. "You look stunning," he said, his eyes widening slightly. Aswathy typically wore sarees only on her birthday, making the unexpected attire a pleasant surprise.

"Ready to visit Tom?" Ali asked, his voice filled with professional enthusiasm.

Aswathy nodded, eager to see Tom's progress. They made their way to the tenth floor, the quiet corridor a stark contrast to the bustling activity of the rest of the hospital.

Upon entering Tom's room, they found the nurses waiting with a dressing tray, a physiotherapist, and a quadrangular walker. Tom was asleep, his best friend, Rohan, sitting quietly by his bedside.

Aswathy's heart ached at the sight of Tom's fragile form. His beard, grown longer during his hospitalization, emphasized his vulnerability.

The sounds of their arrival stirred him from his slumber. He opened his eyes, his gaze immediately locking onto Aswathy. A flicker of recognition, a moment of startled awareness, crossed his face.

Tom's mind, still clouded by medication and the lingering effects of his injuries, struggled to process the scene before him. The radiant figure, glowing and ethereal, seemed to confirm his earlier vision of an angel. The delicate fragrance of jasmine filled his nostrils, a stark contrast to the sterile, antiseptic scent that had permeated his senses for days.

He felt as if he had been transported to another realm, a place of peace and healing.

Dr. Ali's voice, clear and professional, broke through the haze of his thoughts, grounding him in reality. Ali explained the day's procedures: a wound dressing change and the first steps towards mobilization with the aid of a walker.

As the nurses began to carefully remove his bandages, the raw, exposed wounds sent waves of pain through his body. He clenched his jaw, bracing himself against the sharp, searing sensation.

Suddenly, a warm, gentle touch enveloped his hand.

The delicate scent of jasmine filled his senses, a soothing balm to his physical and emotional pain.

In that instant, the searing pain seemed to recede, replaced by a sense of calm and tranquility.

The touch, the fragrance, created a moment of profound comfort, a sense of healing that transcended the physical realm.

"Tom," Dr. Ali said, his voice gentle but firm, "this is Aswathy. Dr. Tom's daughter, and a post-trauma counselor on our team."

He paused, allowing the information to register. "You see," he continued, gesturing towards the healing wounds, "you have very minimal wounds for an intramedullary nailing procedure. Dr. Tom is a very skilled surgeon. Your wounds are healing remarkably fast."

He looked directly at Tom, his eyes conveying a sense of reassurance. "But to heal the fractures completely," he emphasized, "your mind needs to be calm. Stress and anxiety can hinder the healing process. We need to keep you relaxed and positive."

The nurses efficiently changed the dressings, revealing the surprisingly small wounds, a testament to the precision of the surgery.

Next, the physiotherapist stepped forward, her demeanor encouraging. She gently instructed Tom on how to sit up on the edge of the bed and demonstrated the proper use of the quadrangular walker.

Tom, his face etched with determination, attempted to bend his knee. A sharp, excruciating pain shot through his leg, a raw reminder of the recent trauma. He instinctively tightened his grip on Aswathy's hand, his fingers pressing into her palm with a desperate intensity.

Aswathy felt the pressure, the sharp, almost tangible pain radiating from his hand into her own. She winced, her own body echoing his suffering. But she didn't withdraw her hand. Instead, she offered a silent, unwavering support, her touch a grounding anchor in his moment of vulnerability. The shared pain created a strange, unspoken bond between them, a connection that transcended the sterile confines of the hospital room.

With a determined effort, Tom managed to stand, his weight supported by the quadrangular walker. He stood for a few precarious seconds, his body trembling, his face contorted with pain. A wave of dizziness washed over him, and he felt a sudden, terrifying sense of instability, as if he were about to collapse.

Just as he felt himself losing his balance, a steadying hand supported him, guiding him gently back towards the bed.

He was lowered onto the mattress, the relief of horizontal stability washing over him. He turned his gaze towards his savior, his eyes meeting Aswathy's. She offered him a warm, reassuring smile, her eyes filled with gentle encouragement. The smile seemed to dispel the lingering fear and pain, replacing it with a sense of calm.

Dr. Ali, observing Tom's efforts with a satisfied nod, offered a final word of encouragement.

"Excellent progress, Tom," he said, his voice filled with genuine praise. "We'll continue with the mobilization tomorrow. In the meantime, practice your quadriceps exercises. They'll help strengthen your leg and prepare you for more movement." He then turned to leave, his expression conveying a sense of optimism and confidence in Tom's recovery.

XI

Aswathy returned home in the evening, the day's events replaying in her mind. After dinner, she called her father, detailing Tom's mobilization and his progress. As she ended the call, she glanced at her hand and forearm, noticing the faint red marks left by Tom's intense grip. Though she felt no pain, she imagined she could still detect the lingering scent of the hospital, a subtle reminder of the sterile environment.

That night, her dreams were again disturbed. She saw a bandaged, faceless figure riding a horse, trapped in an endless loop, unable to dismount. An overwhelming sense of helplessness washed over her, a desperate urge to assist the figure. But just as she reached out, the shrill sound of an alarm ripped through her dream, jolting her awake.

Since it was her day off, she decided to indulge in a late morning sleep, a rare luxury. Malu Amma, aware of her preference for leisurely mornings on her days off, allowed her to rest undisturbed. She finally woke around noon, joining Malu Amma for a late lunch.

The afternoon was spent rearranging her room, a therapeutic activity that brought a sense of order and calm. She changed the bedsheets, gathered the laundry, and cleaned the room, the familiar tasks grounding her in the present. Alexa played a Taylor Swift playlist, the upbeat melodies filling the room with a cheerful energy.

In the evening, Dr. Ali and his wife visited, a welcome surprise that lifted Aswathy's spirits. Malu Amma prepared a special biryani for dinner, the fragrant spices filling the apartment with a warm, inviting aroma. They spent the evening chatting, catching up on life and sharing stories.

During their conversation, Dr. Ali mentioned Tom's behavior that day. "He was very uncooperative," Ali said, his voice tinged with concern. "He seemed...distracted. He kept asking where you were. He needs your encouragement, Aswathy. He responds well to you."

That night, Aswathy's dreams were once again haunted by the bandaged rider. This time, however, the figure was not trapped on the horse, but rather standing beside it, gazing helplessly upwards. His posture was one of desperate longing, as if waiting for a celestial rescuer, an angel, to descend and offer aid.

The dream was unsettling, filled with a sense of profound isolation and yearning. Aswathy's sleep was fitful, punctuated by fragmented images and a pervasive sense of unease. Time seemed to stretch and distort, each minute an eternity. She lay awake, her eyes fixed on the darkness, feeling as though dawn would never arrive, trapped in the liminal space between sleep and wakefulness, haunted by the rider's silent plea.

The morning finally arrived, bringing with it a sense of release, as if Aswathy had emerged from a dark cocoon into the light of day. After a quick breakfast, she bid farewell to Malu Amma and headed towards the hospital. As she passed the familiar flower stall, she felt an unexpected urge to buy jasmine blossoms, the fragrant white flowers a symbol of the comfort and connection she had felt in Tom's presence.

She waited for Dr. Ali, but he was running late. In the meantime, one of her scheduled patients arrived. However, Aswathy found herself unable to concentrate, her mind still preoccupied with the unsettling dreams and the lingering image of the bandaged rider. She felt distracted, unable to offer her usual level of focused attention. She apologized to the patient, explaining that she was feeling unwell, and rescheduled the appointment for the following day.

Dr. Ali finally arrived, his apologies brief but sincere. They immediately proceeded to the tenth floor, where the physiotherapist was waiting, eager to continue Tom's mobilization.

As Aswathy entered the room, Tom's eyes lit up, a spark of hope igniting within him. His demeanor shifted, becoming more alert and engaged.

The physiotherapy session commenced, and Tom, to his surprise, experienced significantly less pain than the previous day. He attributed the change to Aswathy's presence, the warmth of her smile, the gentle encouragement in her voice. He felt a strange sense of dependence, as if her presence acted as a powerful analgesic, an addictive opioid that eased his physical and emotional suffering.

Rohan sat quietly, observing the physiotherapy session. Dr. Ali, noticing the absence of Tom's mother, inquired about her whereabouts. Tom's demeanor immediately changed. A wave of intense pain washed over him, both physical and emotional. He let out a low moan, his body recoiling from the effort. He retreated to the bed, closing his eyes, shutting out the world.

The fragrant scent of jasmine, which had provided him with such comfort, seemed to vanish, replaced by the sterile, clinical smell of the hospital.

The mention of his mother, the unresolved conflict, the lingering sense of abandonment, had extinguished his newfound hope, draining him of all motivation to walk.

Aswathy observed the immediate and dramatic shift in Tom's demeanor. The mention of his mother acted as a trigger, unleashing a torrent of pain and emotional distress. She recognized the signs: a deep, unresolved conflict, a wound that ran far deeper than his physical injuries.

She understood then that his recovery hinged not only on physical therapy but also on emotional healing. The fractured bones needed to mend, but so did the fractured relationship between mother and son. She realized that her role extended beyond that of a trauma counselor; she needed to become a mediator, a bridge between two wounded souls.

That night, Aswathy called her father. The moment she heard his voice, she sensed an underlying tension, a subtle shift in his usual calm demeanor. "Papa, are you alright?" she asked, her voice filled with concern.

He attempted to reassure her, using the affectionate nickname "Shaari" that he reserved for moments of deep tenderness. "I'm fine, darling," he said, his voice slightly hoarse. "It's just the weather. It's snowing here in Tashkent, and the sudden cold has irritated my throat."

Aswathy, though relieved that it wasn't a serious health issue, insisted he rest his voice and disconnected the call, her mind still preoccupied with the events of the day.

She began to ponder the complex dynamic between Tom and his mother. The medical records provided only basic information: he was an only son, and his mother worked in Noida. Beyond that, there was a void, a silent testament to the unspoken pain that separated them. She made a mental note to speak with Rohan the following day, hoping he could shed some light on the situation.

The next morning, she met with Rohan in her hospital room. He was a childhood friend of Tom, their bond forged in the shared experiences of growing up as neighbors in Noida. "We've been friends since we were kids," Rohan explained, his voice filled with a quiet affection.

He revealed that Tom's mother, Thushara, was a gynecologist at a hospital in Noida. Tom was her only son, and she was a divorcee, having separated from his father before he was even born. Despite the absence of his father, Tom and his mother shared a close, loving relationship.

"They were inseparable," Rohan said, his voice tinged with a hint of sadness. "She sent him to his grandmother's for his higher studies, but after graduation, he came straight back to her."

However, two months ago, Thushara had abruptly left for her native place for two weeks, leaving Tom alone in Noida. During that time, Tom's grandmother passed away. "And then," Rohan continued, his voice dropping to a whisper, "something happened between them. A big argument. He's furious with her. But he won't tell me what it was."

Rohan's inability to explain the root cause of the conflict, increased Aswathy's curiosity. She knew she had to find out what happened.

Aswathy visited Tom in his room, hoping to engage him in conversation. However, he appeared to be sleeping. She hesitated, a suspicion forming in her mind that he might be feigning sleep, avoiding interaction. She decided to leave, respecting his apparent need for solitude.

Later, Dr. Ali informed her that Tom had been uncooperative throughout the day. "He's not making any progress," Ali said, his voice tinged with frustration. "We're planning to discharge him tomorrow. He needs to continue his recovery at home."

A strange emptiness settled over Aswathy as she heard the news. The thought of Tom leaving the hospital, of him disappearing from her daily life, created a sense of unease. She couldn't quite understand her own reaction, the unexpected feeling of loss that accompanied the news of his discharge.

Later that night, Aswathy called her father, hoping to hear his voice, a familiar anchor in her increasingly turbulent emotional landscape. However, his voice was barely a whisper, hoarse and strained from the cold. "Shaari," he managed to say, his voice weak.

"I need to rest my voice."

A wave of concern washed over her. She knew he wouldn't call unless it was important, but his inability to speak freely left her feeling anxious and isolated. She told him to take care and rest. The silence that followed the end of the call felt heavy and profound.

That night, Aswathy's dream returned, a continuation of the unsettling narrative that had been haunting her sleep. This time, however, the rider was unbandaged, his form clear and distinct. He was riding away from her, his figure receding into the distance. Aswathy found herself running after him, her heart pounding with a desperate urgency.

The distance between them grew, the rider's figure becoming smaller and smaller. Just as she felt herself losing hope, she saw a figure in the distance, an elderly woman with outstretched arms, waiting patiently. The rider glanced back at Aswathy, his expression unreadable, and then turned his gaze towards the waiting woman. He hesitated for a moment, and then, with a resolute movement, he steered his horse in a different direction, away from both Aswathy and the waiting figure.

The dream ended abruptly, leaving Aswathy with a profound sense of loss and confusion. The image of the rider, caught between two worlds, two paths, lingered in her mind, a haunting symbol of unresolved conflict and emotional turmoil. She woke with a start, her heart pounding, the dream's unsettling imagery still vivid in her mind.

XIII

Aswathy woke to the sound of rain drumming against the windowpanes, a soft, rhythmic patter that filled the room with a melancholic tranquility. She asked Alexa to play her rainy day playlist, and Kishore Kumar's voice filled the room, singing "Rimjhim Gire Sawan."

The song's poignant melody seemed to mirror her own feelings, a sense of sadness that felt like tears falling from the sky.

The thought of Tom's impending discharge weighed heavily on her mind. She considered taking a day off, seeking refuge in the comfort of her apartment. But a sense of urgency, a need to connect with Tom before he left, compelled her to go to the hospital.

She dressed in a vibrant red salwar kurti, the color a stark contrast to the gray, rainy day. She added a string of jasmine flowers to her hair, the fragrant blossoms a subtle gesture of comfort and connection. Malu Amma, surprised by the unusual floral adornment, offered a curious glance. Aswathy rarely wore flowers to the hospital.

After completing her morning routine, she decided to visit Tom alone, seeking an opportunity for a private conversation. She wanted to understand the source of his pain, to bridge the gap between his silence and her own growing curiosity.

She reached his room, finding him alone. He lay still, his eyes closed. Sensing her presence, he tightened his eyelids, feigning sleep.

Aswathy, recognizing his pretense, didn't call out to him. Instead, she sat quietly beside his bed, gently taking his hand in hers. She began to caress his hand, her touch light and soothing, offering a silent comfort.

After a few minutes, Tom's pretense faltered. He opened his eyes, his gaze meeting hers.

Aswathy met his gaze with a warm, gentle intensity, her eyes conveying a silent understanding. She didn't speak, simply observing his subtle movements, the tension in his jaw, the guarded expression in his eyes. A soft smile played on her lips, deepening the dimples in her cheeks.

Tom's gaze flickered away, a flicker of pain and vulnerability in his eyes. He finally spoke, his voice low and strained.

"Don't...don't smile like that," he said, his words barely a whisper. "Your dimples...they remind me of my mom."

This was the opening Aswathy had been waiting for. She asked softly, "Where is your mom, Tom?"

He hesitated, a moment of silence stretching between them. Then, he answered, his voice tinged with a weary resignation. "She's at work. Her colleague is on maternity leave, so she's covering extra shifts. And...she took some emergency leave a few weeks ago. Getting time off is difficult for her, especially in a hospital."

Tom fell silent again, his gaze drifting away, lost in a sea of unspoken emotions. Aswathy remained seated, her hand still gently holding his, offering a silent presence, a comforting anchor. He felt a strange sense of calm wash over him, as if he had been transported to a world of peace and tranquility. She allowed him time to process his thoughts, to navigate the turbulent waters of his feelings.

A sudden knock on the door shattered the quiet intimacy of the moment, bringing them both back to the harsh reality of the hospital room.

Dr. Ali entered, his eyes widening slightly as he took in the scene: Aswathy holding Tom's hand, their connection palpable. A knowing smile spread across his face, and he offered a playful wink.

Aswathy felt a wave of embarrassment wash over her, her cheeks flushing crimson. She instinctively tried to withdraw her hand, but Tom, startled by Ali's arrival, attempted to sit up. The sudden movement caused his injured leg to twist, sending a jolt of excruciating pain through his body. He instinctively tightened his grip on Aswathy's hand, his fingers digging into her palm with desperate intensity.

"How are you, Tom?" Dr. Ali asked, his voice cheerful, trying to diffuse the awkward tension. "Ready to go home?"

He then turned to Aswathy, his smile broadening. "And Aswathy, how is our patient doing? Is he fit for discharge?"

The playful glint in his eyes suggested he was well aware of the unspoken connection between Aswathy and Tom.

Tom and Aswathy were both momentarily speechless, caught off guard by Ali's direct questions.

They exchanged a fleeting, embarrassed glance, their unspoken emotions hanging heavy in the air.

Just then, Rohan entered the room, oblivious to the charged atmosphere. "We're ready to go!" he announced, his voice enthusiastic. "Tom's mother said she can't make it during the day, so there's no need to wait for her for discharge."

"Alright," Dr. Ali said, his tone efficient and professional. "Then I'll process the discharge papers. The nurse will provide you with the discharge summary, and I'll give you the date for your next follow-up visit. Take care, Tom."

He turned to leave, pausing at the door. "Aswathy, are you coming?" he asked, a knowing smile playing on his lips.

Aswathy, flustered and eager to escape the awkward situation, rushed to join him, her cheeks still flushed.

XIV

Aswathy felt a profound sense of dullness following Tom's discharge, a strange emptiness that lingered despite her efforts to shake it off. Fortunately, she had only two appointments that day, which she managed to complete quickly.

After lunch, she sat in her office, her gaze drawn to the faint red marks on her palm, a lingering reminder of Tom's intense grip. Dr. Ali entered, his eyes twinkling with mischief. "Is it still paining, Aswathy?" he asked, his gaze shifting between her hand and her slightly watery eyes.

"May I offer some remedies?"

Aswathy, startled, wasn't sure if Ali was genuinely concerned or teasing her.

She decided to play it safe, assuming his concern was genuine. "No, thank you, Ali Uncle," she replied, forcing a smile. "It's not painful. Just...lingering."

She then changed the subject, inquiring about her father's work in Tashkent. "How is Papa doing?" she asked.

"He's very busy," Ali replied, his smile fading slightly. "And his sore throat is making things difficult. He might have to extend his stay for a few more days."

A wave of sadness washed over Aswathy. The thought of her father's delayed return amplified her sense of loneliness. She bid Ali goodbye and went straight home, seeking solace in the familiar comfort of her apartment.

Feeling restless and disturbed, she turned to her usual coping mechanism: cooking.

She entered the kitchen and began preparing biryani, a special recipe taught to her by her father. It was their reconciliation meal, a dish he would prepare after their rare disagreements, accompanied by a bouquet of jasmine flowers. The fragrant spices and the shared meal always brought them back together, a symbol of their enduring bond.

Malu Amma sat quietly in the kitchen, observing Aswathy's movements, offering small, helpful gestures. The familiar rhythm of cooking, the chopping of vegetables, the stirring of spices, brought a sense of calm to Aswathy's troubled mind.

Finally, the dum biryani was ready, its aroma filling the apartment with warmth and comfort. They shared the meal, the familiar flavors a soothing balm to Aswathy's troubled spirit.

That night, she called her father, relieved to hear his voice sounding clearer. He confirmed Ali's information, explaining that he had to extend his stay.

He also mentioned missing Tom's post-operative visits. "I feel uneasy not seeing him," he admitted, his voice tinged with concern. "And I'll likely miss his review too."

The next few days were hectic, filled with appointments and consultations. Aswathy immersed herself in her work, finding a temporary distraction from her unsettling thoughts. She tried to convince herself that her intense reaction to Tom was merely a fleeting infatuation, a momentary emotional blip.

Despite her efforts to suppress her feelings, Aswathy found herself increasingly restless as the day of Tom's scheduled appointment approached. She tried to maintain a facade of normalcy, but her sleep was once again plagued by the recurring dream. The bandaged rider, now unbandaged, continued his journey, always choosing a different path, a different direction. He was always moving away from her and the waiting elderly woman, her arms outstretched in a silent plea.

Each variation of the dream amplified her sense of helplessness and confusion. The rider's constant avoidance, his deliberate choice to stray from both her and the waiting figure, created a sense of profound unease. She woke each morning feeling drained and disoriented, the dream's unsettling imagery lingering in her mind.

On the day of Tom's review, Aswathy woke with an uncharacteristic lightness, a sense of anticipation that she couldn't quite explain. Alexa, sensing her mood, played the romantic melody "Na Jaane Mere Dil Ko Kya Ho Gaya" from the film DDLJ, the song's sweet lyrics mirroring her own unspoken feelings.

She freshened up, choosing a navy blue salwar kurti, a professional yet elegant ensemble. She suppressed the urge to wear jasmine flowers, mindful of Dr. Ali's teasing.

In the afternoon, Ali called her to his OPD. As she entered, she saw Tom, accompanied by Rohan.

The absence of Tom's mother was conspicuous, suggesting either she was unable to take time off work, or that the rift between mother and son remained unresolved.

Tom's recovery was progressing rapidly. He could now walk a few meters with the assistance of a walker or crutches, his movements gaining strength and confidence.

When he saw Aswathy, his eyes sparkled with a warmth that was impossible to ignore. Dr. Ali, ever the observant one, exchanged a knowing glance with Aswathy, his smile hinting at the unspoken connection between them.

Ali removed Tom's stitches, confirming the excellent healing. He advised Tom to return for a follow-up review in six weeks.

Aswathy, feeling a sudden urge to escape the charged atmosphere, turned to leave. She noticed Tom's wheelchair and, without a word, began to push it out of the room. Ali, understanding her unspoken desire for solitude, simply smiled and nodded, allowing her to leave.

They walked in silence down the corridor, the rhythmic click of the wheelchair wheels echoing in the quiet space.

Aswathy longed for a moment alone with Tom, a chance to bridge the lingering silence between them. But Rohan's presence, though well-intentioned, prevented any opportunity for private conversation.

As they reached the hospital's exit gate, Rohan suddenly turned to Aswathy.

"Could I get your contact number?" he asked, his voice casual. "Just in case we have any doubts about Tom's rehabilitation."

Tom, though silent, watched the exchange with a subtle amusement, a flicker of something akin to hope in his eyes.

Aswathy, her heart fluttering slightly, gave Rohan her phone number, her gaze lingering on Tom's. She offered him a warm, reassuring smile, a silent promise of continued support.

It was, she realized, both the medicine advised by the doctor and the medicine desired by the patient.

XV

Aswathy waited for Tom's call or message, her phone silent, her anticipation growing with each passing day. Even his WhatsApp status remained unchanged, a blank slate that offered no clues to his thoughts or activities. She tried to convince herself that he was simply busy with his rehabilitation, focusing on his recovery. But a nagging doubt lingered, a suspicion that she was perhaps overthinking, projecting her own feelings onto a situation that might be entirely innocuous.

Her busy schedule offered little time for introspection, forcing her to focus on her patients and her work. Two days later, her father returned from Tashkent. His early morning flight meant he arrived home weary and pale. As soon as he entered, Aswathy rushed to him, enveloping him in a tight, comforting hug.

She noticed his pallor, the subtle signs of exhaustion etched on his face.

"Are you alright, Dad?"

she asked, her voice laced with concern, raising a questioning eyebrow.

He attempted to brush off her concern, attributing his weariness to the overnight flight and his lingering sore throat. But Aswathy, her intuition heightened, hugged him tighter, placing her ear against his chest. She detected a slightly rapid and irregular heartbeat, a subtle irregularity that sent a flicker of unease through her. However, she decided to dismiss it for now, attributing it to fatigue.

After he freshened up and ate breakfast, Tom retreated to his room, seeking the restorative power of sleep. Aswathy, wanting to create a comforting atmosphere, began preparing his favorite lunch: a special dum biryani.

She knew he also loved lemon tea, especially the unique blend he brought back from Uzbekistan. She brewed a pot, adding cloves and cardamom to enhance the flavor, a combination he particularly enjoyed. The fragrant tea had a revitalizing effect on him.

They shared a relaxed lunch, catching up on the events of the past few days. Aswathy carefully avoided mentioning Tom, not wanting to add to her father's fatigue.

He, however, inquired about Tom's rehabilitation, expressing his regret at missing the follow-up appointment. Aswathy reassured him that he could see Tom at his next visit.

In the evening, Ali and his wife visited, their presence a welcome distraction. They discussed the day-to-day happenings at the hospital, while Aswathy, Ali's wife, and Malu Amma chatted in the kitchen, their conversation flowing freely.

Ali and his wife, childless, treated Aswathy as their own, their affection a comforting presence in her life.

After a late-night chat, Ali and his wife departed, leaving Aswathy and her father to retire for the night.

A gentle drizzle pattered against the windowpanes, creating a soft, soothing rhythm. Alexa, sensing the mood, began playing "Rimjhim Gire Sawan," the melancholic melody filling the room.

Tom entered Aswathy's room, finding her still asleep, her expression peaceful. Her phone lay nearby, its screen displaying a WhatsApp profile picture of a young man, a long side profile shot that offered little in the way of identification. Tom's brow furrowed slightly, a flicker of curiosity in his eyes.

The slight movement in the room stirred Aswathy from her slumber. She opened her eyes, finding her father standing beside her bed, her phone in his hand. He handed it back to her, and a thick silence settled between them, the only sound the gentle melody of

Kishore Kumar's voice.

As the next song began, the romantic strains of "Pranayamanithooval pozhiyum pavizha mazha" filled the room. Aswathy, suddenly flustered, quickly called out to Alexa, instructing her to skip to the next track.

She knew her father wasn't particularly fond of the melodic love song, and the sudden blush that crept up her cheeks only amplified her awkwardness.

Tom, sensing her discomfort, offered a gentle "Good morning," his voice calm and reassuring. He then advised her to get ready for the hospital, breaking the tension with a practical suggestion.

The days continued to pass, each one marked by Tom's continued silence. Aswathy's restlessness grew, her irritability reaching a fever pitch. She finally acknowledged the truth she had been trying to deny: she had developed feelings for Tom. However, she was plagued by uncertainty, unsure if her feelings were reciprocated.

Tom, noticing his daughter's unusual mood swings, attributed them to premenstrual syndrome, a simple explanation for her emotional volatility. He offered her extra attention and support, trying to create a calming presence in her life.

He was also preoccupied with his own work, catching up on patient reviews after his absence, requiring him to work extended hours at the hospital.

Almost a month later, Dr. Ali informed Aswathy that Tom was scheduled for a visit the following day. He was experiencing ankle pain and general discomfort.

The mention of Tom's name in front of her father sent a wave of embarrassment through Aswathy, and she quickly excused herself, leaving the room.

That night, Aswathy's mind raced with unanswered questions. Why hadn't Tom contacted her? Would she have an opportunity to speak with him alone the next day? Had he reconciled with his mother? Her sleep was fitful, disturbed by a restless energy.

After a long absence, the dream of the horse rider returned. This time, the rider moved towards the waiting elderly woman, his gaze fixed on her. However, he stopped midway, his posture filled with hesitation. The shrill sound of the alarm clock jolted Aswathy awake.

She looked out the window, seeing the first rays of dawn painting the sky. She made morning tea and called her father, noticing his fatigue.

Tom, still drowsy from sleep, felt unusually tired. Aswathy attributed it to his recent return to work, the demanding schedule taking its toll.

Over tea, Tom explained his exhaustion, attributing it to the increased workload. He mentioned that he might be late for work or take the morning off to rest.

Aswathy prepared for the hospital, choosing a vibrant red churidar, the color a bold statement against the morning's grayness. She adorned her hair with fragrant jasmine flowers, their delicate white petals a stark contrast to the deep red of her attire. A touch of light makeup enhanced her natural beauty, creating a radiant glow.

Tom, observing his daughter's stunning appearance, couldn't help but admire her. A soft smile played on his lips, his eyes filled with paternal affection. When she smiled back, her dimples deepened, amplifying her charm and highlighting her inner joy.

Tom lingered in his room after breakfast, the lingering headache prompting him to take a paracetamol. Around 11 AM, he decided to head to the hospital.

He went directly to the canteen, ordering a strong cup of tea, hoping the caffeine would alleviate his headache. After finishing his tea, he walked towards his office.

As he approached the exit, he noticed Aswathy, her demeanor animated and cheerful, conversing with a young man seated in a wheelchair. A sleek car pulled up, and a beautiful woman emerged.He only saw the back of the lady.

With Aswathy's assistance, the young man transferred into the car. Tom observed Aswathy's gentle care, the way she supported the young man, her touch both firm and reassuring. He assumed the woman was the young man's mother.

Suddenly, a wave of dizziness washed over Tom. He felt a strange warmth at his nostril, a sensation he couldn't quite place. He leaned against the nearby wall, seeking support.

After the car drove away, Aswathy turned and saw her father, his hand pressed to his nose, taking deep breaths. She noticed his pallor and the slight tremor in his hands.

Concerned, she walked towards him. He, in turn, looked back at her, a faint smile playing on his lips, and then continued towards his office.

In his office, Ali was waiting. "The young Tom you operated on before going to Tashkent just left after his review," Ali informed him. "He's recovering well."

Tom nodded, his gaze lingering on Aswathy, who seemed lost in her own thoughts. He noted her distant expression, her eyes unfocused, as if she were in a dreamlike state.

XVII

During dinner, Aswathy's cheerful demeanor persisted, a rare and welcome sight. She hummed softly, her voice filled with a melodic lightness. Tom, still puzzled by her sudden change in mood, observed her with a quiet curiosity.

He inquired about her day at work, and she blushed, a subtle flush that heightened her natural beauty. She then spoke of Tom (the younger one), mentioning his improved mood but also revealing the ongoing tension between him and his mother.

"They're not speaking at home," she said, her voice tinged with concern. "But they maintain a civil relationship in public."

After dinner, they retreated to their respective rooms. Tom, his headache still lingering, took a sleeping pill, hoping to find some respite.

The following days passed, and Aswathy's cheerful disposition remained constant. Tom, having recovered from his initial fatigue, resumed his normal work routine.

However, he remained perplexed by his daughter's sudden and sustained good mood, wondering about its underlying cause.

The next few days passed uneventfully, a quiet rhythm of work and home life. Then, one morning, Aswathy received a "good morning" message from Tom.

She nearly jumped out of her skin, her heart pounding with an unexpected surge of excitement. A blush warmed her cheeks, and she reread the message, a silly grin spreading across her face.

She replied with a simple "good morning" and "how are you," her fingers trembling slightly as she typed. A wave of giddiness washed over her, and she felt her legs weaken, prompting her to lie back on the bed, her mind filled with a dreamy haze.

The rest of the day was spent in a similar state of blissful distraction. Tom, observing his daughter's dreamy demeanor, found it amusing, a subtle shift in her personality that he couldn't quite explain.

The exchange of "good morning" messages continued for a few days, a simple ritual that brought a quiet joy to Aswathy's mornings. However, the messages remained brief, lacking any substantial progression.

Then, one day, Tom messaged, complaining of pain and redness at the screw site on his right leg. Aswathy, her concern overriding her shyness, promptly replied, urging him to visit her father. She assured him that she would arrange an emergency appointment.

The following day, Tom arrived at the hospital, and Dr. Tom examined him for the first time since the surgery.

Aswathy accompanied Tom to her father's office, her presence a silent source of support. Dr. Tom, after a thorough examination, suspected an underlying infection. He advised Tom to be admitted for further observation and ordered blood tests.

Upon hearing the recommendation for admission, Aswathy's eyes sparkled with an undeniable joy, a reaction that was both unexpected and revealing. Tom and Ali exchanged a thoughtful glance, their expressions hinting at a silent understanding of Aswathy's true feelings.

Tom was admitted to the same room on the tenth floor, a familiar space that now held a different significance for Aswathy. He was placed on intravenous antibiotics and other medications to combat the suspected infection.

The blood test results arrived in the afternoon, confirming Dr. Tom's suspicions. Tom's white blood cell count was elevated, and his C-reactive protein (CRP) levels were also high, indicating an active infection.

In the evening, Aswathy visited Tom, bringing a plate of banana fritters, a comforting treat they had shared before. They ate in silence, the quiet atmosphere filled with unspoken emotions.

Aswathy longed to break the silence, to initiate a conversation, but the words seemed to elude her, trapped in the labyrinth of her unspoken feelings. She finished her banana fritters and left the room, leaving Tom alone with his thoughts and the beeping of the hospital monitors.

The following day, Aswathy visited Tom before her father's scheduled rounds. She wore a vibrant yellow salwar kurti, the color radiating warmth and cheerfulness, and adorned her hair with jasmine flowers, their delicate fragrance filling the room.

When Dr. Tom arrived for his patient rounds, he immediately noticed the lingering scent of jasmine. He realized that Aswathy had visited Tom earlier, a subtle gesture that spoke volumes about her feelings.

He found himself grappling with a sense of confusion, unsure of how to navigate the delicate situation. He wondered how far this budding relationship would progress, and whether he should intervene, speaking to Aswathy or Tom directly. He was caught between his paternal concern and a desire to respect their growing connection.

XVIII

Aswathy took the afternoon off, deciding to go home. Tom, meanwhile, was in surgery, unaware of her absence.

Upon arriving home, she went straight to the kitchen, seeking solace in the familiar rhythm of cooking. She decided to prepare "ilayada," a sweet dish made from rice flour, a comforting treat that always brought her a sense of peace.

She began by making the dough, mixing rice flour with hot water until it formed a smooth, pliable texture. Setting the dough aside, she prepared the filling, grating coconut and mixing it with sugar. She then heated banana leaves, gently bending them to soften them.

Taking a portion of the dough, she flattened it onto a banana leaf, creating a thin, even layer. She placed two spoonfuls of the coconut filling in the center and folded the dough over, sealing the edges to form small dumplings. She steamed the ilayada in an idli steamer until they were cooked through.

After sampling one, she smiled, satisfied with the perfect balance of sweetness and texture. She packed several ilayada and brewed a flask of black tea, infused with cloves and cardamom, a fragrant and comforting beverage. She then headed back to the hospital, to Tom's room.

Tom was alone, lying on the bed. He sat up when he saw Aswathy, offering a quiet "hi." Aswathy blushed, returning the greeting. An awkward silence settled between them.

Finally, Aswathy broke the silence, offering him the ilayada and tea. Tom's expression shifted, a mix of happiness and sadness flickering across his face.

"My mom used to make this for me as an evening snack," he said, his voice tinged with melancholy.

The mention of his mother brought a wave of sadness, a reminder of their strained relationship.

Aswathy, sensing his emotional turmoil, asked gently, "What happened between you two, Tom?"

He hesitated, his gaze searching hers. But the genuine concern in her eyes prompted him to open up.

"My mother and grandmother were my only family," he began, his voice low. "I always thought she was divorced.

Whenever I asked about my father, she'd change the subject, her eyes filled with sadness. Eventually, I stopped asking. But seeing other children with their fathers, I always felt a sense of loss."

"A few weeks ago," he continued, "my grandmother became ill at our native place, and my mother went to see her."

"She rushed to my grandmother and took her to the hospital," Tom continued, his voice heavy with emotion. "But my grandmother was old and had multiple health issues."

"Two days later, my mother called, asking me to come to my grandmother's." He paused, his gaze distant. "She was in the ICU, nearing the end."

"My grandmother called for both of us," he said, his voice trembling slightly. "She started to ramble, talking about a letter my father had sent to my mother, asking for kindness. She mumbled a lot of other things too, things I couldn't quite understand."

"That night," he went on, "I asked my mother about my father again. She remained silent."

"Finally," he said, his voice barely a whisper, "I asked her if she had ever been married. I'd never seen a wedding album, or any pictures of my father. She got angry and slapped me."

"The next day," he continued, "my grandmother died. After the funeral rituals, we returned home."

"Two days later," he said, his voice filled with a raw intensity, "I was at Rohan's house, watching him interact with his parents. Seeing their love, I called my mother again and asked about my father. I was irritated, and I asked her if I was a bastard."

"She became extremely angry," he said, his voice breaking.

"She cursed me, told me to go to hell. I got into my car and drove straight into a wall." He finished his story, his gaze fixed on the floor, the weight of his pain hanging heavy in the air.

Tom began to cry, his tears a release of the pent-up pain and confusion he had carried for so long. Seeing his vulnerability, Aswathy's own eyes welled up with tears. She felt a profound sense of sadness, a deep empathy for his suffering.

Unsure how to comfort him, she stood up and moved closer. He instinctively leaned into her, burying his face in her chest, seeking solace in her warmth. Aswathy held him tightly, gently patting his back, offering silent comfort.

Time seemed to stand still, the silence broken only by the soft sound of Tom's tears. He eventually stopped crying, his body still trembling, his mind lost in a haze of emotion.

The sudden ring of Aswathy's phone startled them, breaking the intimate moment. It was her father, calling to inquire about her location. She told him she was at the hospital and would be heading home soon.

Tom, his voice hoarse, said he was also leaving and would wait for her at the exit.

That night, Aswathy found herself enveloped in the lingering scent of Tom, a subtle fragrance that clung to her clothes and filled her senses.

It was a comforting presence, a reminder of the vulnerability he had shared, the emotional connection they had forged. She drifted off to sleep, a sense of peace settling over her.

Her dream returned, the familiar image of the horse rider appearing once more. This time, however, the rider moved towards her, covering a few meters of the distance that had always separated them.

The slight shift in direction, the subtle movement towards her, filled her with a sense of hopeful anticipation, a feeling that the long journey was finally beginning to change course.

XIX

The next day, Tom's blood test results returned to normal. Dr. Tom declared him fit for discharge, announcing that he could go home the following afternoon.

Aswathy's mood shifted again, a subtle sadness clouding her eyes. Dr. Tom, noticing her reaction, also observed a similar melancholy in Tom's demeanor.

Tom asked his son if his mother would be visiting, expressing a desire to meet her. Tom replied that he had informed her, and she would likely come, as she wanted to personally thank the surgeon who operated on her son.

At dinner, Tom noticed Aswathy's distant, dreamy state. He understood her emotional turmoil and decided to let her process her feelings in her own time, without interruption.

The following morning, Aswathy woke early, determined to prepare another special dish for Tom. She also planned to give some to his mother, remembering her father's words about the power of food to connect with people's hearts.

She decided to make unnakkaya, one of her father's favorite snacks. She began by steaming ripe bananas, then peeling and deseeding them. She mashed the bananas into a smooth dough.

Next, she prepared the filling, sautéing nuts, almonds, and raisins in ghee. She added sugar, cardamom powder, and a pinch of salt.

She flattened portions of the banana dough, filled them with the nut mixture, and shaped them into elongated ovals. Finally, she deep-fried the unnakkaya until golden brown.

She packed some for Tom and placed a few on the breakfast table for her father and herself.

Tom, seeing the unnakkaya, smiled, appreciating her thoughtful gesture. He found the sweetness of the snack particularly intense that morning, attributing it to the unspoken affection between them. He offered her a playful smile but remained silent.

They went to the hospital together. During his usual room visit, Dr. Tom informed Tom that he could go home in the afternoon and left the room with Ali.

Aswathy handed the packed unnakkaya to Tom, asking him to share some with his mother.

In the afternoon, Dr. Tom was called for an emergency surgery, a complex procedure that left him exhausted. As he walked towards his office, he saw Aswathy saying goodbye to Tom's mother. He only saw her from the side but he noticed Aswathy's raised hand.

Suddenly, he felt a wave of dizziness and a warm sensation in his nostril. He pressed his fingers against his nose and was shocked to see bloodstains.

He leaned against the wall and quickly entered his office.

Aswathy, after seeing Tom and his mother off, turned to find her father gone. Surprised, she went to his office.

She found him sitting there, his face pale and tired. He explained that the surgery had been particularly difficult.

That night, Tom messaged Aswathy, his words filled with a quiet gratitude. He told her that his mother had enjoyed the unnakkaya, and that they had talked for a while. The simple act of sharing the sweet treat had created a bridge, a moment of connection between them.

Aswathy, her heart filled with a gentle warmth, replied, reassuring him that everything would eventually work out. She then wished him a good night, her words a silent promise of support and hope.

XX

The following days were marked by Tom's continued messages to Aswathy, each one a subtle update on the evolving relationship with his mother. He shared that their bond was slowly returning to its former state, though a lingering hesitancy, a subtle step backward, always remained.

As their communication increased, their connection deepened. Tom began to call her more frequently, their conversations flowing easily, filled with shared laughter and quiet understanding. Yet, neither of them explicitly expressed their feelings, their unspoken affection hanging in the air, a delicate, unspoken promise.

Tom's frequent mentions of his mother sparked a sense of curiosity within Aswathy. She had only a faint memory of her own mother, who had passed away before her first birthday. All she had was a single photograph, a faded image of her mother holding infant Aswathy, her face radiating a warm, loving smile. She noticed the dimple on her mother's cheek, a feature she had inherited. The realization that Tom's mother also had a dimple, a shared physical trait, filled her with a strange sense of connection.

One night, during dinner, Aswathy decided to broach the subject of her mother with her father. She noticed an immediate shift in his demeanor, a subtle tension that filled the room. He understood that she was seeking answers, that the questions she had held within her for so long were finally demanding to be heard.

Seeing her father's prolonged silence, Aswathy understood that he was grappling with a difficult decision. She sensed a reluctance, a hesitation to reveal the information she sought.

Suddenly, he rose from the table, his movements abrupt. "I have a severe headache," he said, his voice strained. He pressed a tissue against his nostrils, a gesture that struck Aswathy as odd, unrelated to a headache.

She felt a surge of frustration, a suspicion that he was using his discomfort as an excuse to avoid her questions. However, she also knew her father's character.

He had always been a man of his word, assuring her that he would reveal the truth about their family when the time was right. She clung to that promise, trusting that he would eventually fulfill it, just as he had fulfilled all his other promises.

With a sigh, she resigned herself to waiting, hoping that the "right time" would arrive soon. She retreated to her room, the unanswered questions lingering in the silence.

The next morning, Aswathy prepared tea and went to wake her father. He was still asleep, his breathing deep and even. As she entered his room, she noticed a crumpled tissue lying on the floor. Usually, her father was meticulous about keeping his room tidy.

She picked up the tissue to discard it, but her eyes widened as she noticed the dark, dried bloodstains. A wave of fear washed over her. She immediately called out to him, her voice trembling.

He opened his eyes slowly, his expression calm. She looked at his face, noticing the dried bloodstains near his nostril. Her heart pounded in her throat, and she began to cry, her voice choked with emotion. "What's wrong, Dad?" she asked, her voice pleading.

He looked at her, his expression a mask of confusion. She showed him the bloodstained tissue, and his face paled. He initially tried to deflect, offering a weak explanation.

"I...I accidentally scratched the inside of my nostril with my nail while cleaning it," he stammered. "That's why there's blood."

His explanation sounded unconvincing, even to his own ears. Aswathy's eyes, filled with tears and suspicion, held him captive.

He then changed his approach, adopting a more practical tone. "I'll visit an ENT surgeon today," he said, "just to make sure there's no lingering injury."

He reached out, taking both of Aswathy's hands in his, his touch gentle and reassuring. She, overwhelmed by a wave of emotion, leaned against him, seeking comfort in his familiar warmth. She placed her ear against his chest, listening to the rhythm of his heartbeat. A flicker of unease washed over her as she noticed a subtle irregularity, a slight deviation from the steady, rhythmic pulse she was accustomed to. The irregularity made her even more nervous.

XXI

At the hospital, Tom went directly to his ENT colleague, insisting on going alone, telling Aswathy that she had waiting appointments. At lunchtime, father and daughter met in his office, joined by Ali.

Tom explained that a minor vessel in his nostril had been injured and cauterized. Ali then added that Tom's blood pressure was slightly elevated, and his heavy workload at the hospital was contributing to his fatigue. Ali suggested that Tom take a few days off.

Tom readily agreed, and then suggested to Aswathy that she also take some leave, proposing a trip together the next day.

Aswathy felt a mix of excitement and sadness. She was thrilled at the prospect of spending quality time with her father but also felt a pang of disappointment at the thought of missing Tom (the younger one).

Her father went home after lunch, and Aswathy stayed at the hospital to apply for leave, starting the next day. She then messaged Tom (the younger one), explaining the situation and advising him to focus on supporting his mother.

Tom was recovering well, both physically and emotionally, thanks to the improved relationship with his mother.

He had started preparing tea for her, following Aswathy's recommendations, which helped her relax after work.

These small gestures created opportunities for them to talk, further strengthening their bond.

At the dinner table, Aswathy eagerly discussed the travel plans with her father. To her surprise, he had already made arrangements. He outlined a simple itinerary: a trip to Kerala for a few days.

He had already booked their flight tickets and arranged for a self-driven car. He mentioned that their accommodation could be flexible, allowing them to explore different places at their own pace.

Malu Amma would stay back at their current home. It would be just the two of them, a father-daughter getaway.

Aswathy's heart fluttered with excitement at the prospect of visiting Kerala. A wave of anticipation washed over her, intertwined with a deeper hope. She hoped that in the land of her roots, surrounded by familiar sights and perhaps even familiar stories, she might finally learn more about her mother.

After dinner, she eagerly began packing her clothes. Tom, observing her enthusiasm, advised her to pack light.

"We can always buy anything you need there," he suggested, his voice gentle, perhaps sensing her underlying yearning for connection to her past.

As Aswathy settled into bed, she called Tom, sharing the news of their upcoming trip. "We're going to Kerala," she said, her voice filled with a mix of excitement and a hint of underlying yearning.

She recounted their only previous visit, a fleeting memory from when she was ten years old, for her grandmother's funeral.

"That's the only time I remember going," she added.

"I don't even know if we have any relatives there anymore. Dad never talks about our native place, or about Mom. Whenever I try to ask, he just goes silent."

Aswathy slept soundly, a sense of hopeful anticipation filling her dreams. She woke up early, eager for the journey to begin.

Despite Malu Amma's capable nature, Aswathy meticulously went over all the household instructions, ensuring everything was in order for their absence.

Their flight was scheduled for the evening from New Delhi to Kozhikode. After a quiet day spent preparing, they bid farewell to Malu Amma and headed to the airport.

The flight landed smoothly at Kozhikode International Airport. Their pre-booked self-driven rental car was waiting for them. After completing the necessary formalities, they set off towards Kozhikode city, where they planned to spend the night.

They checked into their hotel, had a quiet dinner in their room, and Tom retired early, still feeling the effects of his recent health scare. Aswathy messaged Tom (the younger one) to let him know they had arrived safely and then tried to sleep.

However, her excitement kept her awake, her mind buzzing with anticipation for what the trip might reveal. She finally drifted off to sleep in the early hours of the morning.

XXII

The sun ascended in the eastern sky, its gentle morning rays casting delicate shadows across Aswathy's face through the windowpane. She stretched, a feeling of unexpected energy coursing through her despite the few hours of sleep.

She gently woke her father, and they shared a cup of tea she brewed in their room. Refreshed, they changed into new clothes, a sense of anticipation hanging in the air. Tom announced it was time to check out.

After a leisurely breakfast at the hotel restaurant, they loaded their luggage into the rented SUV and began their journey. Aswathy, her curiosity piqued, asked their destination for the day.

"Just wait and see," Tom replied with a mysterious smile. "Tell me if any of this looks familiar."

Tom navigated without the aid of map applications, relying on his memory and instincts. He connected his phone to the car's audio system via Spotify, and his favorite playlist filled the car with familiar melodies.

Aswathy gazed out the window, observing the unfolding scenery. She knew Kozhikode was considered the largest city in the Malabar region. Compared to the sprawling metropolis of Delhi, Kozhikode felt smaller, yet vibrant and growing.

She noticed the abundance of food stalls and restaurants, bustling with people, a testament to the city's reputation for its culinary delights.

The roads, though well-maintained, were mostly single-lane, winding through the landscape with considerable traffic. After an hour's drive, Tom pulled over at a roadside hotel for a tea break.

He offered Aswathy a banana fry, its golden-brown exterior tempting. She took a bite and was instantly impressed by its deliciousness, even declaring it better than Malu Amma's.

Refueled by the tea and snack, they continued their leisurely drive. Aswathy, unable to contain her curiosity any longer, repeated her question about their destination.

"We're heading to my native place," Tom finally revealed.

"It's located on the eastern side of Kozhikode, a place called Kakkadampoyil." He explained that it was a hilly region, recently gaining popularity as a tourist destination.

The ongoing construction of a new highway caused some diversions along their route. By lunchtime, they reached Kakkadampoyil town.

They decided to have lunch at a small hotel run entirely by women, its signboard proudly displaying the name "Kudumbasree Vanitha Hotel."

The lunch at the Kudumbasree Vanitha Hotel was a delightful experience, simple yet bursting with authentic flavors. The waitress placed a fresh green banana leaf in front of Aswathy and offered a small jug of water. Aswathy, remembering local customs, sprinkled a few drops of water on the leaf.

The waitress then presented the day's offerings: crisp banana chips, a vibrant cabbage thoran (a dry vegetable dish with coconut), aviyal (a medley of vegetables in a coconut-yogurt sauce), a crunchy pappadam, and two curries – a fragrant sambar and a rich, red fish curry. They also ordered a plate of karimeen fry, a local delicacy of pearl spot fish.

The meal was exceptional. The karimeen fry was incredibly tasty and fiery, so much so that Aswathy felt tears welling up in her eyes and a slight tingling in her nostrils.

To cool the palate, they were offered "porridge water" (the starchy water left after cooking rice), a surprisingly refreshing and traditional drink.

Aswathy had never experienced a lunch quite like it; she savored every bite. The meal concluded with a sweet and creamy semiya payasam (vermicelli pudding), a perfect ending to the flavorful spread.

After their satisfying lunch, Tom inquired about accommodations in the area, specifically those convenient for an early morning visit to Kurisumala, a nearby hill known for its pilgrimage site and scenic views.

They found a small guesthouse nestled amidst the lush greenery of Kakkadampoyil. The guesthouse offered simple but comfortable rooms, and its balcony provided a breathtaking panoramic view of the surrounding hills. They checked in, leaving their luggage in their room.

Tom suggested a short drive to a nearby waterfall, a popular attraction in Kakkadampoyil. Aswathy readily agreed, eager to explore the natural beauty of the region.

The drive was short, and they soon arrived at the waterfall, its cascading waters creating a refreshing mist in the air. They spent some time enjoying the scenery, the sound of the falling water a soothing backdrop to their conversation.

As the sun began to set, they returned to the guesthouse, had a simple dinner, and retired for the night, looking forward to their early morning visit to Kurisumala.

Aswathy tried to call Tom before going to sleep, wanting to share the details of their day and their plans for the next morning. However, the mobile network signal in their remote location was weak and intermittent. The guesthouse's Wi-Fi, unfortunately, didn't reach their room.

Frustrated but understanding of the limitations in a hilly area, Aswathy decided to wait until they reached a stronger network signal the next day to contact him. Despite the lack of connectivity, the peaceful surroundings and the day's experiences lulled her into a comfortable and deep sleep.

XXIII

Aswathy awoke to the symphony of nature, the stillness of the pre-dawn air punctuated by the diverse calls of unseen birds. She remembered their plan for an early morning trek to Kurisumala.

She gently roused Tom, and after a quick brush, they changed into tracksuits and trekking shoes, stepping out into the cool darkness.

The trek was a mere 1.5 kilometers. However, at the trail's entrance, a line of jeeps idled, their drivers offering their services. They explained that the initial half of the route was a treacherous jeep track, best navigated by their sturdy vehicles before the actual trekking began. Tom decided to take the jeep.

They settled into the front jeep, and the bumpy ride commenced. The road was riddled with potholes, and Aswathy held on tightly, the jostling surprisingly enjoyable.

For a fleeting moment, she imagined riding a horse along this rugged path with Tom (the younger one), a smile blossoming on her face.

Her father noticed her smile and raised an eyebrow in silent inquiry. She simply shrugged, her smile lingering.

At the end of the jeep track, they disembarked and began their ascent. Though still dark, there was enough ambient light to discern the trekking trail. They were the first to venture out that morning, father and daughter climbing slowly in comfortable silence. The first rays of the sun began to paint the eastern sky with hues of orange and pink.

After about forty-five minutes of steady climbing, they reached the summit. A large concrete cross stood sentinel against the dawning sky. They sat beneath it, catching their breath.

Tom was breathing heavily, his heart pounding. He closed his eyes, taking deep, deliberate breaths, settling into a moment of quiet meditation.

Aswathy, seeing her father's peaceful state, gazed around. The vista that unfolded before her was breathtaking. As the sun climbed higher, the lighting became magnificent, revealing a 360-degree panorama of rolling green hills. She felt a profound connection to the land, a sense of being truly in "God's Own Country."

Suddenly, Tom opened his eyes and pointed to a distant outline of a building. "That's a church," he said, his voice soft, "and our old home was near it."

He then began to speak of his family history, a narrative Aswathy had long yearned to hear.

"My father and mother came to this area with the dream of farming," he began. "They were originally from South Kerala. At that time, this land was mostly barren, and people came here seeking ample space for cultivation. The population was sparse, and connection to the outside world was difficult, with almost no transportation services."

"Both my parents started farming and built their life here. My mother gave birth eight times, but only me survived. All my siblings died at a very young age due to the lack of accessible medical care."

"The loss of their children deeply affected them," Tom continued, his voice tinged with sadness. "They became determined that I would have a better life, that I would become a doctor. So, they poured everything they had into my education. We had no relatives here, and I didn't have any friends either. My only focus was my studies."

"When I was fifteen," he said, his voice dropping, "my father died from a snake bite. He didn't receive the medical attention he needed in time. After my tenth standard, I went away to college, staying in a hostel and only visiting my mother on weekends."

"I have no relatives left here, and after Mom's death, I tried to forget this place entirely," Tom confessed, his voice filled with remorse. "That's why I've always been silent about it all. I'm really sorry, Shaari."

He paused, taking a deep breath as they began their descent. "I handed over the property documents of our place to the church after Mom passed away," he added quietly, the weight of his past evident in his tone.

They continued their walk down the hill, the silence between them now carrying a different weight, one of shared understanding and unspoken emotions.

XXIV

They returned to their guesthouse, the morning's trek having worked up a healthy appetite. After a satisfying breakfast, Aswathy spent some time by the swimming pool, enjoying the refreshing water. Around noon, they checked out and began their drive back towards Kozhikode, stopping for another delicious lunch at the Kudumbasree Vanitha Hotel.

As they neared the city, the heavens opened, and a steady rain began to fall. Tom, behind the wheel, turned on his playlist.

The familiar strains of "Rimjhim Gire Sawan" filled the car. "This was Soorya's favorite song," Tom said softly, the first time he had mentioned his late wife by name in a long while.

Aswathy listened quietly, sensing the shift in his mood. He seemed lost in thought, driving in silence as the melancholic melody played.

They reached the Palayam old bus stand area. Just as the playlist transitioned to "Pranayamanithooval pozhiyum pavizha mazha," Aswathy instinctively reached to change the song.

"Wait," Tom said gently, stopping her hand. "It all started here, and this song was playing in the background."

Aswathy's heart skipped a beat. She thought he was about to tell her the story of how he met her mother, Soorya.

Tom simply gestured towards the bustling bus stand. "Everything has changed so much in all this time," he murmured, a hint of nostalgia in his voice, before starting the car again.

"After my pre-degree days," he began, his gaze fixed on the road, "I passed the common entrance test for medical college admission. Before starting college, I would often come to this area to watch movies. It was a kind of pent-up desire, maybe like the K-drama binge-watching you do nowadays." He chuckled softly. "Some Sundays, I'd see four films back-to-back."

"One day, I was sitting on the bus to go home. It was raining, and the sounds of songs drifted from the music cassette shops around the Palayam bus stand.

A light drizzle was falling, and I was enjoying the raindrops on my face when my eyes fell on a beautiful girl waiting for her bus. She was under the shelter of an umbrella, but the rain still kissed her face. She had the cutest dimple, just like yours. She was wearing a half-saree."

He paused, a soft smile gracing his lips. "It was love at first sight. Suddenly, she looked up and our eyes met. I felt like I'd been electrocuted. My bus started moving just then, and she was lost from my view."

"The melody of 'Pranayamanithooval' played in my mind over and over," Tom continued, his voice soft with the memory.

"I looked back at the spot where she had been standing, but she was gone, swallowed by the crowd and the rain. I honestly never thought I would see her again."

He paused, navigating the car through the heavy Kozhikode traffic. He pointed out various eateries along the way. "That was where we used to get the best samosas during college," he'd say, or "Ah, that tea shop made the strongest ginger tea." Each place held a small piece of his past, a silent testament to the life he had lived before Aswathy.

The evening crowd in Kozhikode was overwhelming, a chaotic mix of people and vehicles. Finally, Tom navigated through the throng and reached a hotel situated right by the beach.

After checking in, both of them immediately headed towards the shore. For Aswathy, who had spent her entire life in Delhi, a visit to a real beach, with the vast expanse of the ocean stretching out before her, was like a dream come true. The beach was teeming with people, their voices and laughter mingling with the rhythmic crashing of the waves. The salty air filled her lungs, a stark contrast to the dry, dusty air of Delhi. She gazed in wonder at the endless horizon, the setting sun painting the sky in vibrant hues of orange, pink, and purple.

The beach was a vibrant hub of activity, lined with numerous small shops offering a tempting array of local delicacies.

Aswathy's eyes widened at the sight of the various food items. There were mounds of steamed green peas, baskets of boiled chicken and quail eggs, and the renowned kallummakaya (mussels) prepared in various ways.

Colorful displays of mango slices, carrot sticks, and pineapple chunks glistened, sprinkled with salt and chili powder. Ice cream carts offered a multitude of flavors and colors.

She was particularly fascinated by a vendor meticulously shaving ice from large blocks into a glass, then inserting a stick to create a simple yet refreshing ice lollipop. The air was filled with the enticing aromas of spices and the sweet scent of tropical fruits.

Aswathy's enthusiasm bubbled over. "Oh my goodness!" she exclaimed, her eyes darting from one tempting treat to another.

"You should have told me we were coming to a place like this! If I had known, I definitely would have skipped lunch!" She gestured animatedly at the array of snacks, her stomach already rumbling at the sight and smell of it all. "I want to try everything!"

Aswathy, unable to resist the tempting spread, ordered a small portion of almost every item that caught her eye. They found an empty bench facing the vast expanse of the Arabian Sea, the gentle sound of the waves providing a soothing backdrop to their culinary adventure.

Tom watched Aswathy with a tender smile, his eyes filled with affection as she enthusiastically sampled each snack, her face alight with delight at the explosion of flavors. The setting sun cast a warm golden glow on her face, highlighting her happiness.

"The sea has certainly encroached upon the shore more," Tom observed, his gaze sweeping across the water.

"I remember this area having plenty of trees back then. Seems like everything has been uprooted."

He then pointed towards a dilapidated structure extending into the sea. "See that sea bridge, now ruined? It was in good condition back then. And there was a tea seller right at the end of it.

He made the most amazing Sulaimani, that black tea, with a dash of 'ishq' – love, or maybe just a secret ingredient," he added with a nostalgic smile.

"I never thought I'd witness the same captivating beauty I saw at Palayam again in my life,"

Tom continued, his voice soft, his gaze distant as he looked at Aswathy. "But life, as you said, is full of surprises."

He turned his gaze back to the sea, a reminiscent smile playing on his lips. "There she was, sitting in the first class of our MBBS program. And there it was again... that mesmerizing dimple, smiling right at me."

He chuckled softly, a hint of youthful infatuation in his tone. "My heart skipped a beat, and in my mind, I could almost hear 'Pranayamanithooval' playing in the background once more."

Aswathy's breath hitched. "Shaaru?" she repeated, the name unfamiliar yet strangely resonant. She had always believed her father was recounting his first encounter with her mother, Soorya. She had never heard anyone call her mother by the pet name "Shaaru."

Seeing the bewildered look on Aswathy's face, Tom chuckled softly. "No, no," he clarified. "She wasn't the Soorya I eventually married. That's another story altogether. Shaaru and I... well, we shared plenty of Sulaimani from that little shop near the sea bridge, along with some wonderfully tasty snacks."

As darkness enveloped the beach, they began their walk back to their hotel room. Aswathy, still full from their seaside feast, declared she wouldn't need any dinner.

"Tomorrow," Tom said, a hint of a smile in his voice, "I'll show you some of the places in Kozhikode where Shaaru and I... where we built our bond."

Back in their room, Tom was quiet, the memories of his past seemingly drawing him into a contemplative silence. He soon fell asleep.

Aswathy, however, was still buzzing from the day's discoveries. She called Tom (the younger one) and excitedly shared the experiences of the last two days, recounting the journey to Kakkadampoyil and their evening at the beach. They talked for a while before finally saying good night.

The next morning, Tom greeted Aswathy with a wide smile.

"Today," he announced, "we are going on a culinary adventure!"

They started their day early, heading straight for Hotel Paragon, a renowned restaurant in Kozhikode. There, they indulged in a traditional Kerala breakfast of soft, lacy appam, delicate neypathiri (thin rice pancakes), flavorful chicken kuruma, and spicy fish mulakittath (red chili fish curry).

Between bites, Tom continued to share his memories of Shaaru.

"We were the best of friends," he recounted, a fond smile gracing his lips. "We helped each other immensely with our studies. Shaaru had the most beautiful handwriting, and her lecture notes were exceptional. Almost everyone in our class would borrow them to study."

He described their days spent walking through the college corridors, poring over books together in the library, and sharing lighthearted conversations on the college grounds. They also reminisced about their visits to SM Street strolling through the bustling shops, and later relaxing by the Mananchira Square, sipping juice from nearby vendors. He pointed out Bombay Hotel, where they often enjoyed a delicious biriyani, and recalled their occasional trips to the cinema together.

"But we never confessed any romantic feelings,"

Tom admitted, a hint of melancholy in his voice. "We were such close friends, and perhaps both of us were afraid of jeopardizing that. Being from different religious backgrounds also made us wary of potential complications. We feared that taking the next step and failing would mean losing our precious friendship."

As they walked through the now less crowded SM Street, Tom pointed out landmarks and shared anecdotes of their time there. After their biriyani lunch at Bombay Hotel, they spent the evening sampling various snacks from Hotel Zain, another local favorite.

XXVI

The next day, their destination was Munnar, a famous hill station known for its sprawling tea plantations and breathtaking scenery. They started their journey early in the morning, leaving the coastal plains of Kozhikode behind.

As they drove, the landscape gradually transformed. The air grew cooler and fresher as they ascended into the Western Ghats.

Lush greenery enveloped them, with rubber plantations and spice gardens dotting the hillsides. Tom pointed out various spice plantations, explaining the cultivation of cardamom, cloves, and pepper.

Aswathy gazed in awe at the changing scenery, the winding roads offering panoramic views of valleys and distant peaks. The aroma of spices hung heavy in the air, a sensory delight. They stopped occasionally to admire waterfalls cascading down rocky cliffs and to capture the picturesque landscapes with their cameras.

Tom shared stories of his college days, but the narrative of Shaaru seemed to have reached a natural pause. Aswathy didn't press him, sensing that he was perhaps lost in his own thoughts, the memories of his past mingling with the beauty of their present journey. The drive to Munnar was a visual feast, a tranquil transition from the bustling city to the serene embrace of nature's grandeur. They anticipated reaching Munnar by late afternoon, eager to explore the tea estates and mist-covered hills.

"After our MBBS, we said our goodbyes," Tom continued, his voice tinged with a hint of regret.

"I still remember the look in her eyes when we last met. I was almost certain she would say yes... to whatever unspoken feelings lingered between us. But I wasn't ready. I wasn't sure about the future, about the potential obstacles our different backgrounds might present."

He sighed softly. "I took up a temporary job at a tea estate hospital in Munnar after graduation. It was a quiet place, and it gave me plenty of time to prepare for my postgraduate entrance exams. This was a time before mobile phones, email, or social media, so contacting Shaaru was difficult, almost impossible."

Tom's narration continued as they drove along the Gap Road towards Munnar. The scenery was breathtaking, a tapestry of rolling hills carpeted in vibrant green tea bushes, the mist clinging to the higher slopes like a soft veil. Aswathy gazed out the window, captivated by the sheer beauty of nature at its finest. The winding road offered stunning vistas at every turn, making it one of the most picturesque drives she had ever experienced. The air was crisp and cool, carrying the fresh scent of tea leaves and eucalyptus.

They reached Club Mahindra Munnar, a resort nestled amidst the verdant hills. After checking in and settling into their comfortable room, they decided to unwind by the pool, the cool water a welcome contrast to the journey.

Later, after enjoying a refreshing evening tea, Aswathy finally had a moment to call Tom (the younger one). She hadn't been able to reach him the previous night as her father had been awake and in her company.

She eagerly recounted the past two days, describing their visits to Kakkadampoyil and Kozhikode, the delicious food, and the poignant stories her father had shared, including the tale of his close friendship with Shaaru during their college years. She spoke with enthusiasm, her voice filled with the wonder of the places she had seen and the emotions evoked by her father's memories.

"Later, after a few months in Munnar, once I had settled into my routine, I decided to visit her hometown,"

Tom continued, his voice tinged with a wistful sadness as they sat at the dinner table in the Munnar resort. "I wanted to see her, to perhaps understand why things had remained unspoken between us."

He paused, taking a sip of water. "But when I inquired about her, I learned that Shaaru's wedding had already taken place. It was with a son of a family friend, someone her parents had likely arranged for her. I also found out that her father had passed away, and now she and her mother had moved away from their native place. Since she was also an only child, the neighbors didn't have many details about where they had gone."

A shadow of what might have been flickered across Tom's face. "That was the end of that chapter," he said softly, his gaze distant. "Life, as it often does, took us on different paths."

XXVII

The next morning, Tom gently woke Aswathy before sunrise, suggesting an early walk. The air was crisp and cool, carrying the dampness of the night. They strolled out of the resort, and Tom pointed towards a serene expanse of water in the distance – the Anayirangal dam. They walked in comfortable silence, absorbing the tranquil beauty of the awakening landscape. A thick fog hung low, obscuring the distant hills and creating an ethereal atmosphere.

They reached the banks of the dam, and Tom indicated a cluster of smooth rocks near the water's edge. As they sat down, the first rays of the sun began to pierce through the fog, casting a soft, diffused light that painted the scene in dreamlike hues.

Suddenly, Tom broke the silence. "This is the place where I first met Soorya," he said softly, his gaze fixed on the water. "There was a group of college girls who had come here on a trip. She was sitting on those very rocks, her face etched with pain. She had sprained her ankle while walking."

He turned to Aswathy, a gentle smile on his face. "I noticed her beautiful face immediately, and then... the dimple. A dimple so similar to yours, and to Shaaru's."

"As a doctor, my instincts kicked in," he continued.

"I approached them and offered my help. I advised them to visit the hospital where I was working later that day."

"When she came to the hospital, her ankle was significantly swollen, and she was in immense pain. I admitted her and applied a Plaster of Paris slab to immobilize her leg. By the next morning, her pain had subsided considerably."

"Her warden told me that they were here for an NSS camp. Soorya, despite her injury, was described as an energetic and helpful member of the group."

Tom's voice softened further. "The warden also mentioned that Soorya was an orphan. I felt an immediate pang of pity for her, and her dimple... it kept reminding me of Shaaru."

"We met again in Munnar after that," he explained.

"Her orphanage was located not too far from the tea estate where I was working. My mother, back home, was putting pressure on me to get married. Perhaps out of a sense of loneliness, a lingering echo of my feelings for Shaaru, and a genuine compassion for Soorya's situation... we ended up getting married."

"Later, looking back, I often thought our marriage was rushed," Tom admitted, a shadow of regret crossing his face.

"Sometimes, I wondered if my feelings for Soorya were more of an infatuation, perhaps fueled by that dimple, a constant reminder of Shaaru. It wasn't fair to Soorya, I realize that now."

He paused, his gaze drifting towards the distant hills. "A few months after our wedding, my mother told me that a lady had come to our home, asking for me. From her description, I immediately knew it was Shaaru. A wave of 'what ifs' washed over me. I couldn't help but think that if I had waited just a little longer, perhaps Shaaru and I..." He trailed off, leaving the sentence unfinished, the unspoken possibility hanging heavy in the cool morning air.

"But despite those lingering thoughts, I never intentionally tried to hurt Soorya," Tom said, his voice earnest.

"She was a kind and understanding soul. She knew about my past, about Shaaru, and she always tried her best to soothe my restless heart. When she became pregnant with you, an opportunity arose for her to come to Uzbekistan. I also found a good job here, and so we moved. A few months later, you, my little Shaari, came into our world. With your arrival, slowly but surely, the memories of Shaaru began to fade, replaced by the overwhelming joy and love I felt for my wife and my daughter."

The next two days in Munnar were filled with exploration and shared moments. They wandered through sprawling tea estates, the emerald slopes stretching as far as the eye could see. They visited Mattupetty Dam, its still waters reflecting the surrounding hills, and Echo Point, where their calls reverberated through the valleys. They breathed in the fragrant air of spice gardens and marveled at the vibrant blooms.

Upon their return to Delhi, Aswathy continued her nightly calls with Tom (the younger one), sharing the stories of their trip. Tom (the elder) was aware of these conversations but chose not to intrude, respecting Aswathy's privacy.

Tom extended his leave for another week, while Aswathy rejoined work the next day. Life settled back into its familiar rhythm, the days passing smoothly. Months went by, and Tom's fractures were healing steadily.

However, the relationship between Tom and his mother remained strained, a subtle distance persisting despite their occasional interactions.

One night, after one of Tom's follow-up appointments, Aswathy was chatting with her father about the ongoing tension.

"They're still not completely normal, are they?" she observed, a hint of concern in her voice.

Suddenly, Tom (the elder) interjected with a mischievous glint in his eyes. "Tell Tom to make a biriyani and serve it with a glass of

Sulaimani filled with 'ishq'."

Aswathy laughed. "Dad, I don't think that's going to magically solve everything."

Tom chuckled. "Well, tell him to at least add some cloves and cardamom to his mother's tea, like you do. And maybe... just maybe...send him the recipe of your biriyani."

Aswathy relayed her father's advice to Tom (the younger one) during their nightly call, and he chuckled heartily.

"Biriyani?" he exclaimed. "You know I'm a complete novice in the kitchen! My culinary repertoire extends to a few snack items, and even those aren't exactly gourmet creations."

He admitted that the few times he had attempted Aswathy's snack recipes, the results were far from superb. The idea of him suddenly conjuring a delicious biriyani, let alone one imbued with 'ishq', seemed hilariously improbable to both of them.

After much playful persuasion from Aswathy, Tom (the younger one) finally agreed to attempt making biriyani. They decided to discuss the intricacies of the recipe during his next hospital visit.

Aswathy also informed him about her upcoming trip to Uzbekistan with her father, mentioning that they were scheduled to leave the day after his appointment. The news added a layer of anticipation to their next meeting.

On the day of Tom's appointment, he had a scheduled leave, allowing him and Aswathy some time alone before her father arrived for his rounds. Aswathy seized the opportunity to explain the steps for making the biriyani and the special tea in detail. She emphasized preparing it for dinner that evening.

Additionally, she suggested a thoughtful gesture: to buy some fresh jasmine flowers and place them on his mother's dressing table in the morning, a subtle way to create a pleasant atmosphere before the evening's culinary endeavor.

Tom's fractures had healed considerably, allowing him to walk without the aid of crutches. That night, Tom (the elder) and Aswathy boarded their flight to Tashkent, embarking on their journey to Uzbekistan.

Two days after his conversation with Aswathy, Tom (the younger one) finally decided to put her plan into action. While his mother was taking a bath before heading to the hospital, he carefully placed the fragrant jasmine flowers on her dressing table.

When she emerged, she noticed the delicate white blossoms and a soft smile touched her lips. She gently tucked them into her hair and offered Tom a warm, genuine smile as she said goodbye, a silent acknowledgment of his thoughtful gesture.

Seeing this first step met with such a positive reaction, Tom felt encouraged to proceed. He ordered all the necessary ingredients for preparing biriyani. By 7 PM, a fragrant and colorful biriyani was ready on the dining table.

When his mother returned from the hospital, she went straight to her room to freshen up. As she stepped out of the washroom, the rich, savory aroma of biriyani filled her nostrils.

Tom called out to her, "Mom, dinner is ready."

She walked to the dining table and saw the beautifully arranged biriyani. Without a word, she sat down and began to eat. They shared the meal in a comfortable silence. After finishing, she retreated to her room.

A few moments later, Tom gently knocked on her door. He held out a steaming cup of Sulaimani. His mother looked at the tea, a flicker of curiosity in her eyes.

She took the cup and sipped. The warmth of the tea, infused with the subtle spices, seemed to carry a deeper warmth – the unspoken love of her son.

Tom looked at her, his eyes filled with sincerity. "Mom," he said softly, "I am truly sorry for the harsh words I spoke to you. Please forgive me."

In that moment, the wall that had stood between them for so long crumbled. She felt as though her world had returned to its axis, her son finally back in her embrace, not just physically, but emotionally.

She reached out, gently holding his arm, and they fell into a warm, heartfelt hug, a silent promise of healing and renewed love.

They stood embraced for several minutes, the silence filled with unspoken emotions – relief, regret, and a burgeoning sense of peace. Finally, his mother broke the quiet, her voice soft but clear.

"I studied my MBBS in Kozhikode," she began, her gaze distant, lost in the memories of her youth.

"After completing my course, I returned home. I was the only child of my parents, and their expectations weighed heavily on me. In college, I had a best friend. We were incredibly close, and I often wondered if his feelings for me went beyond friendship. But we never spoke of it, never dared to cross that invisible line."

She paused, a hint of sadness in her eyes. "Then, suddenly, my father had a severe heart attack. In the midst of the fear and uncertainty, he pleaded with me to marry my childhood friend, the son of our family friends.

It was a rushed proposal, fueled by his fragile health. I wasn't ready for marriage, and I certainly couldn't envision him as my life partner. To me, he was like a brother. But my father insisted, his emotional state in the ICU a powerful form of blackmail I couldn't resist."

Her voice trembled slightly as she continued. "I tried to talk to my fiancé, to explain that I couldn't see him as my husband, that my heart wasn't in it.

He just smiled, dismissed my concerns, and threw himself into the wedding arrangements, as if my feelings were irrelevant."

A deep sorrow etched itself onto her face. "On our wedding night... he forced himself on me. It shattered something within me. I felt utterly broken, violated. In my despair, I tried to end my life."

Her voice cracked, and tears welled in her eyes. "My parents and his parents were shocked, devastated. The trauma was too much for my father; his already weakened heart couldn't bear it, and he died.

My in-laws, who had been close family friends for years, were furious with their son. He confessed that his actions were fueled by alcohol and the misguided advice of his friends. He fled, terrified, knowing I was in the ICU after my suicide attempt and that my father had passed away."

She took a shaky breath. "Later, my in-laws also moved away. I never tried to contact them again. The pain was too deep, the betrayal too profound."

"Later," she continued, her voice barely a whisper, "when I found out I was pregnant with you, I was devastated. It felt like another burden, a constant reminder of that night. I even visited my college friend, hoping for some solace, but I learned that he too had married."

She sighed, a deep weariness in her expression. "Eventually, I tried to bury all those painful memories, to build a life for us, just the two of us. That's why I never told you anything about your biological father."

"When we went to see your grandmother in her final days, she told me that my husband had gone abroad and died in a hospital as a destitute. I was afraid... afraid that you would blame me for not telling you the truth about your father, about everything. I was terrified of losing you too. That's why I kept quiet all these years. I am so, so sorry." Her voice broke, tears finally spilling down her cheeks.

A faint smile touched his mother's lips, a warmth replacing the earlier sorrow. "But tell me, son," she asked gently, a teasing lilt in her voice, "who put this biriyani idea into your head? I'm quite certain it wasn't your own culinary genius at work."

Tom blushed, a sheepish grin spreading across his face. "Well... there is someone," he admitted, his eyes sparkling. "I'll introduce you to her one day, for sure. She's out of town at the moment."

XXX

The day following their heartfelt conversation passed uneventfully for Tom and his mother, a quiet understanding settling between them.

That evening, during dinner, his mother broached a sensitive topic.

"Son," she began hesitantly, "do you... do you wish to perform the religious rituals for your father, as his son?"

Tom took a long time to answer, his gaze distant as he wrestled with the question.

After a period of deep contemplation, he finally spoke. "Yes, Amma," he said softly. "We will go to Varanasi and do it... for the sake of it. Perhaps a journey will also help to ease some of the lingering weight."

His mother nodded in agreement, and the next day, they traveled to the holy city of Varanasi, where Tom fulfilled his filial duties.

They returned home the following day, the shared experience creating a new layer of understanding between them. Tom messaged Aswathy, recounting all the recent developments.

The next morning, at breakfast, his mother surprised him with a direct question. "So, have you proposed to your girlfriend yet?"

Tom blushed crimson, stammering slightly. "No, Amma. I... I haven't really had the chance. And I'm not even sure if she feels the same way."

His mother looked at him with a gentle wisdom in her eyes.

"Tom," she said softly, "if you love this girl, do not hesitate to convey your feelings. If you don't, you may regret it later. You see," she continued, a wistful smile touching her lips, "if I had confessed my feelings to my best friend in college... perhaps things would have turned out very differently for me." She paused, her gaze meeting his. "But then," she added, a hint of warmth in her voice, "I wouldn't have you, would I?"

Tom's reply was immediate, tinged with a hopeful anticipation. "Mom, she's currently in Uzbekistan with her father. But when she returns, I'll definitely try."

Hearing the name Uzbekistan, his mother fell into a profound silence. Her eyes seemed to glaze over, her expression shifting to one of distant sorrow. After a long, heavy moment, she finally spoke, her voice barely a whisper. "Tom... do you know the place, Samarkand, in Uzbekistan?"

Tom frowned, a sense of unease creeping into his heart. "Yes, Amma, I've heard of it. It's a beautiful, ancient city, isn't it?"

His mother's gaze remained fixed, her voice trembling slightly as she delivered the devastating truth. "Your father... he died there, Tom. He was buried in Samarkand."

"There is a cemetery called Shah-i-Zinda," his mother continued, her voice heavy with the weight of years of unspoken grief. "Your father is buried there."

The revelation hung in the air, a silent thunderclap. Tom stared at his mother, his mind reeling, trying to reconcile the image of his father, a man he barely remembered, with a grave in a faraway land. He felt a strange mix of shock, confusion, and a sudden, unexpected sense of loss for a father he never truly knew.

He didn't say a word. The weight of his mother's confession was too heavy, too sudden. He simply stood up and walked back to his room, the silence in the house amplifying the turmoil within him. He sat on the edge of his bed, his thoughts a chaotic jumble. The desire to visit his father's burial place warred with the longing to see Aswathy.

In Tashkent, Tom immersed himself in his hospital duties, the familiar demands of his profession providing a sense of routine in a new environment. Aswathy, on the other hand, found herself with ample time to explore the Uzbek capital on her own. She discovered a city with a unique charm, a blend of Soviet-era architecture and modern European influences, with wide boulevards and meticulously manicured parks.

She wandered through bustling bazaars filled with vibrant textiles and fragrant spices, visited historical sites adorned with intricate tilework, and savored the local cuisine at cozy cafes.

Her evenings with her father were quiet, their conversations often centered around his work and her day's discoveries. She tried to reach Tom (the younger one), her heart carrying a mixture of anticipation and uncertainty about their connection.

However, he informed her that he was on a trip to Varanasi, and he didn't elaborate further on the details or the duration of his travel.

After a few days, Aswathy's father's work concluded. He announced their next destination: Samarkand, a city renowned for its stunning Silk Road architecture and rich history. Aswathy readily agreed, a flicker of curiosity sparked by the name, unaware of the profound significance it held for someone she cared for deeply.

The next day, they set off towards the ancient city, the landscape unfolding before them with promises of new sights and experiences.

The air in Samarkand was heavy with moisture, a light drizzle painting the ancient stones with a sheen of dampness. Tom (the elder) seemed lost in a deep reverie, his usual cheerful demeanor replaced by a quiet contemplation. They checked into their hotel and decided to rest for the remainder of the day, the journey having left them both feeling slightly weary.

Later, as they settled into their room, Tom's voice held a mix of excitement and a poignant sadness. "This is it, Shaari," he said softly, looking around as if seeing ghosts of the past.

"This very city... I visited it with Soorya, your mother, when she came here for her studies."

His gaze drifted, a melancholic smile touching his lips. "And... this is also the city where she passed away. She's buried here, in a place called Shah-i-Zinda." The realization hung in the air, a heavy, unspoken connection between the city's ancient beauty and a personal tragedy.

That night, Aswathy tried to contact Tom through WhatsApp, but her messages went unanswered. Feeling concerned, she recorded a short voice clip, letting him know that they had arrived in Samarkand.

The next morning, the weather turned unusually cold, and the forecast predicted snow. Tom felt a chill and noticed blood stains on his nostrils. He discreetly masked it from Aswathy's view and told her he would rest for the morning while she explored Samarkand on her own.

Back in Delhi, Tom cautiously broached the subject of visiting Samarkand with his mother. After some hesitation and gentle persuasion, she reluctantly agreed to accompany him to his father's graveyard. Tom tried to downplay the emotional significance of the trip, telling his mother that it was purely out of filial duty and that he harbored no particular sympathy for his deceased father.

The next day, they arrived in Tashkent. Tom made his way to the hospital where Aswathy's father had been working, hoping to connect with her.

However, he learned that both Aswathy and her father had already left Tashkent to explore other parts of Uzbekistan. His attempts to contact her were unsuccessful. With a sense of resignation, Tom decided to proceed to Samarkand with his mother and figure things out from there.

XXXII

Aswathy ventured out to explore the wonders of Samarkand on her own. The city unfolded before her like a living history book, its turquoise domes and intricate tilework whispering tales of the Silk Road. She stood in awe at the grandeur of the Amir Timur Mausoleum, its towering presence a testament to a bygone era. The Bibi Khanum Mosque, despite its partially ruined state, still evoked a sense of majestic scale.

At lunchtime, she called her father, who said he was resting at the hotel. She returned, and as they ate, Tom casually inquired about Tom (the younger one).

"How is he doing in Delhi?" he asked. Aswathy blushed, admitting that she hadn't heard from him in the last two days.

Tom looked intently into her eyes. "Has he proposed to you yet?"

A deeper blush spread across Aswathy's face, and she shyly hid it with her hands. "No, not yet," she mumbled, adding with a hint of uncertainty, "and I'm not even sure if he... if he loves me."

Her father's advice was immediate and heartfelt. "Aswathy, if you truly love him, don't wait for him to make the first move. Meet him when you return to Delhi, and tell him how you feel."

Aswathy suddenly lost her appetite, her thoughts consumed by her father's words. She excused herself and went out again.

After lunch, she decided to visit the Registan Square. The ancient plaza buzzed with activity, despite the chilly weather. Couples sat on benches, their hushed conversations blending with the murmur of the crowd.

A wave of longing washed over Aswathy. She realized she couldn't wait any longer to see Tom. She resolved to ask her father to return to Delhi the day after their planned visit to her mother's tomb. She wanted to visit that significant place with him.

Near the square, numerous flower stalls displayed a riot of colors and fragrances. Aswathy found an empty bench and sat down, lost in thought, her heart filled with a mixture of anticipation and nervousness.

Suddenly, a man approached and sat on the bench opposite her. She didn't immediately register his face, feeling a fleeting sense of awkwardness at the intrusion. She stood up, intending to walk away.

Just then, she heard someone call her name. She turned back, her breath catching in her throat.

Kneeling before her, a bouquet of vibrant flowers in his outstretched hand, was Tom.

The moment Tom knelt, the first delicate snowflakes began to fall. They danced in the air, small white crystals swirling around them, a silent, magical backdrop to the unfolding scene.

Aswathy stood frozen, a wave of disbelief washing over her. She didn't know what to do, her body trembling uncontrollably.

Was it the sudden drop in temperature, the biting cold seeping through her clothes? Or was it the sheer anxiety, the overwhelming surprise of Tom's unexpected appearance? Or perhaps, it was the electrifying realization that the man she had been longing for was kneeling before her, a bouquet in his hand, the unspoken question hanging heavy in the snowy air.

She shivered, caught in a whirlwind of emotions, her heart pounding in her chest.

"Aswathy," Tom said, his voice filled with a warmth that seemed to cut through the cold air and the swirling snow,

"I love you. And I need you with me for the rest of my life." He was smiling, a broad, genuine smile that reached his eyes, and Aswathy felt a warmth spread through her chest, chasing away some of the chill.

The world around them seemed to fade, the falling snow creating a soft, hushed intimacy. Aswathy stood there, speechless, her mind struggling to catch up with the reality of the moment. It felt like an eternity had passed, though it was likely only a few precious seconds.

Finally, Tom chuckled softly, a hint of playful discomfort in his voice.

"Please," he added, still smiling, "accept my bouquet. My knees are hurting a bit; I'm still recuperating from those major surgeries, you know."

The lighthearted reminder of his recent ordeal grounded the moment, making it feel both real and incredibly tender.

A blush bloomed on Aswathy's cheeks as she awkwardly reached out and took the bouquet, her fingers brushing against Tom's. She immediately helped him to his feet, her concern for his recovery overriding her initial shock.

Once he was steady, she spontaneously threw her arms around him, a silent expression of the emotions that had been building within her.

They sat down together on the snow-dusted bench, the vibrant flowers a splash of color against the white backdrop. They gazed into each other's eyes, a comfortable silence settling between them. In that shared look, amidst the gentle snowfall of ancient Samarkand, their hearts spoke volumes, conveying a depth of feeling that words could not yet articulate. The world around them seemed to fade away, leaving only the connection in their gazes.

The initial silence soon gave way to a torrent of words, a rush of emotions and unspoken feelings finally finding voice. They spoke of their longing, the uncertainties they had harbored, and the joy of this unexpected reunion in such a faraway land.

Time seemed to melt away as they poured their hearts out to each other, realizing with a pang that their time together was, indeed, limited.

Tom then shared the poignant story of his recent trip to Varanasi with his mother, the unexpected revelation about his father's death in Samarkand, and their planned visit to Shah-i-Zinda.

He spoke of his mother's grief, his own complex emotions towards a father he never knew, and the sense of closure he hoped to find at his final resting place. The shared vulnerability deepened the bond between them, the ancient city bearing witness to their intertwined stories.

Lost in their conversation and the surreal beauty of the snowy setting, they were jolted back to reality by the insistent ringing of Aswathy's mobile phone. It was her father calling. With a sigh, Aswathy told him she would be back at the hotel room soon.

She turned back to Tom, her eyes filled with a bittersweet mixture of joy and reluctance. "I have to go," she said softly. "But I promise, we'll meet again tomorrow... with my father." The unspoken implication hung in the air, a silent acknowledgment that their relationship was about to take another significant step.

XXXIII

Aswathy returned to their hotel room, her face radiant. Her father, though looking tired from the day's explorations, brightened instantly at her happy demeanor. He smiled warmly as she rushed to hug him, her excitement palpable.

"Appa!" she exclaimed, "I met Tom! He proposed!" She held out the bouquet of flowers, a vibrant splash of color in the room. Tom (the elder) beamed, showering her with blessings.

"That's wonderful, my dear! Tomorrow, after we visit your mother's graveyard, we'll offer our blessings for your future together."

Then, Aswathy shared a surprising revelation. "Appa," she said softly, "Tom's father... he's also buried there, in the same place."

They shared a quiet dinner, the news creating a poignant connection to the land they were in. Later, Tom (the elder) retired to sleep, while Aswathy excitedly recounted every detail of her meeting with Tom to her father.

In his own room, Tom (the younger one) had already shared his joyous news with his mother. They were both overjoyed, their hearts filled with hope for his future. After dinner, he called Aswathy, and they talked late into the night, their voices filled with happiness and anticipation.

The next morning, a pristine blanket of white snow covered the entirety of Samarkand as Aswathy and her father made their way to Shah-i-Zinda.

The ancient necropolis stretched far along the hillside, a breathtaking tapestry of intricately tiled mausoleums and varied headstones. Despite being a graveyard, the atmosphere was serene, the fresh snow lending an air of peaceful slumber rather than despair. Beautiful plants and flowers peeked through the white layer, adding touches of color to the tranquil scene.

They walked silently along the snow-covered walkways, searching for Soorya's tomb.

"For a final resting place," Her father murmured, breaking the silence, "this is a good place."

Aswathy shot him an irritated glance. "Appa! Don't talk like that," she chided gently.

Finally, they found Soorya's tomb. They knelt, placing a flower on the cold stone.

Aswathy closed her eyes, offering a silent prayer for her mother and asking for blessings on her relationship with Tom. Her father sat beside her, lost in his own tranquil thoughts.

After a while, Aswathy rose and began to explore deeper into the necropolis, not wanting to disturb her father's quiet contemplation. He remained kneeling, his eyes closed in peaceful reflection.

When Tom finally opened his eyes, Aswathy was no longer beside him. He waited on a nearby bench, watching the occasional visitor wander through the snow-covered tombs. He then noticed a young man and an elderly lady carefully reading the names on the headstones, walking further into the graveyard. The lady looked vaguely familiar.

After some time, he heard Aswathy's voice. She was returning, accompanied by the two people he had just seen.

Suddenly, a wave of disorientation washed over Tom. It was as if he were dreaming, transported back to the bustling Palayam bus stand. There was no rain, but soft snowflakes were falling, and walking towards him, a radiant smile illuminating her face, was a woman with a captivating dimple. His Shaaru.

Tom's mother also looked towards the bench where the man was sitting. A sense of familiarity tugged at her memory, a faint echo of a face from the past. Her steps grew slower and slower as she approached, her eyes fixed on him. Finally, she stopped directly in front of Tom (the elder), her expression a mixture of surprise and a dawning recognition.

A soft smile spread across both their faces, a silent acknowledgment of a shared history.

Aswathy, sensing the unspoken connection, called out to her father. "Appa," she said, her voice filled with a gentle understanding, "you know your patient, Tom? Well, this is his mother."

A look of realization washed over Tom (the elder)'s face. He looked at the elderly woman, his smile widening. "Thushara," he completed, the name a soft murmur, a whisper from a long-forgotten time.

The air crackled with a sudden, unspoken energy. Aswathy looked from her father's softened expression to the gentle smile on the elderly woman's face, a wave of curiosity washing over her.

Then, like a sudden flash of lightning, the truth illuminated her mind. Aunty... Shaaru... The pieces clicked into place, the stories her father had shared, the lingering emotions – it all converged. The woman standing before them, Tom's mother, was the Shaaru of her father's college days.

Aswathy's widened eyes and subtly changed expression didn't escape Tom's notice. He, too, watched the silent exchange between his mother and Aswathy's father. The years melted away, leaving behind the undeniable truth of their intertwined past.

A sudden wave of discomfort washed over Aswathy's father. He instinctively placed a hand over his chest, a pained expression flickering across his face as he slowly sat back down on the bench. He reached out and gently took Thushara's hand, his grip surprisingly firm.

"Shaari," he said, his voice a little strained but filled with a gentle warmth, "I am... happy that Tom is your son. It was fate, wasn't it? Bringing him to my operation theater. And I think," he added, a faint smile touching his lips, "I did a fantastic job. Looks like... I found a good man... for little Shaaru."

Aswathy's eyes widened in alarm as she noticed a trickle of blood flowing from her father's nostril, staining his pale skin. He, too, seemed to sense it, his gaze softening as he looked at her.

"Aswathy, my dear," he said, his voice growing weaker but remaining calm, "don't worry. I am happy now... that you've found the right man." He took a shallow breath. "For the past few months... I was diagnosed with an aneurysm of the aortic arch. I believe... it has ruptured."

His eyes drifted towards the peaceful rows of tombs. "I said earlier... I am happy to sleep here for the rest of my life. And I am also... happy that I met Shaari... at last." A faint smile lingered on his lips, his grip on Thushara's hand loosening.